THE ENDING
is the BEST PART

Lamia Zain is an Egyptian-British author and content creator. When not reading and writing infectious romance, she works in TV. On her TikTok account @lamia.reads, she has cultivated a vibrant, engaged group of followers who supported her as she wrote *The Ending is the Best Part* for the 'BookTok Made Me Write It' project. This book is her love letter to the BookTok community.

THE ENDING is the BEST PART

LAMIA ZAIN

CORVUS

Published in paperback in Great Britain in 2025 by Corvus,
an imprint of Atlantic Books Ltd.

10 9 8 7 6 5 4 3 2 1

A CIP catalogue record for this book is available from the British
Library.

Paperback ISBN: 9781805464976
E-book ISBN: 9781805464983

Printed in Great Britain by Clays Ltd, Elcograf S.p.A.

Corvus
An imprint of Atlantic Books Ltd
Ormond House
26–27 Boswell Street
London
WC1N 3JZ

www.atlantic-books.co.uk

Product safety EU representative: Authorised Rep Compliance Ltd., Ground Floor, 7
1 Lower Baggot Street, Dublin, D02 P593, Ireland. www.arccompliance.com

MIX
Paper | Supporting
responsible forestry
FSC® C018072

To all the hopeless romantics...

Chapter One

This is it. Things are finally looking up for me. Sure, I've had a few knockbacks, like my ex-boyfriend Theo cheating on me and getting into a relationship with the girl he did it with, but I'm basically over that. Even if it has been two – okay, three years since it happened. Oh, and then there was that whole thing of almost setting my flat on fire. Can I just clarify the *almost* in that scenario? I may or may not have forgotten to turn the stove off. But the thing is ancient, and like everything else in the flat my landlord refuses to replace it. I mean there wasn't even a full-blown fire, just a few flames and a burnt wooden spoon, so does it even count?

My dating life might be in shambles and my housing situation is less than ideal, but professionally I am truly living my best life at twenty-five years old. Not to blow my own horn, but I am working my dream job as a junior staff writer on one of the most successful television shows of all time,

Claim to Power. You know the one. It's got dragons, fairies, kings and queens in it. And an epic storyline full of high-stakes battles and political intrigue, not to mention the slow-burn enemies-to-lovers plot that's been building up over the last few seasons. You can thank me for that particular detail.

And today, my boss has called me in for a one-on-one meeting. She only does that to fire people or promote them. I know I haven't done anything that would cause me to get fired and I'm not going to lie, work has been going pretty well recently. The senior writers keep asking for my input on how to resolve this or that detail on the show. They say I'm good on character. I understand relationships – I told my mum all that time reading Austen and the Brontës wasn't a waste. If only that knowledge could extend to my personal life.

Anyway, all of us know that the season finale needs to be written, and someone needs to take the lead. That someone could be, might be, me.

I love my job. I'm writing on a show that's watched by millions and it's a really supportive workplace. All those stories you hear about ultra-competitive writers' rooms? Well, thankfully that hasn't been my experience. I like all my co-workers. Well, all except for one. But I have good reason, because he is genuinely one of the most insufferable people I have ever met.

Xander. The other junior writer and my number one enemy at work. You might think having a 'number one enemy' is a little dramatic, but no. Not for him. He's your classic pretentious posh boy. A film bro who'll only talk about 'the greats': Scorsese, Nolan and Tarantino. Don't get me wrong, I like their movies as much as the next person with a MUBI subscription, but we can all have a laugh about Tarantino's foot thing and agree that time Scorsese directed a musical was a Big Mistake. Xander looks down on everything I like: Emily Henry, Bridget Jones and Richard Curtis. He said he hadn't even heard of Nora Ephron – and somehow the man claims to love film. It's 2025 and this guy has no social media presence except for Letterboxd, not that I stalked him or anything...

I'll admit he's a great writer. It's undeniable. Unfortunately. He can imbue even the quietest moment with a drama that pretty much no one else can. He's brilliant in the storyboarding sessions too. When it comes to battle scenes and coronations, deaths and complex political manoeuvres, he's your guy. But he says he doesn't get the point of romance. It's all just fluff, according to him, a distraction from the 'proper' narrative, which probably explains why I always get called in to help him with his scenes that have *any* character development.

But soon, none of that is going to matter. Because I have a meeting with my manager Meagan McLean. You may have heard of her – multiple BAFTA winner and showrunner of *Claim to Power* and a hundred other huge TV shows. She's kind of my hero. I love how she creates a team spirit among her writers. She's obsessed with the idea that a healthy balance of competition and collaboration creates TV magic. And hey, it works. Look at the heights she's climbed. Heights that I'm hoping to follow her to.

If she gives me the lead screenwriter credit, I'll be able to get any writing gig I want. Maybe someone will finally commission me to write the throwback nineties rom-com I've always dreamed of. Then, I'll barely even remember Xander when I'm giving my Oscars speech. I wonder what I'll wear? What if I trip on my dress like Jennifer Lawrence? That would be mortifying – and, unfortunately, just like me.

Stop. I'm getting ahead of myself. It's fine, it's going to be fine. Let's ignore all that, because today is going. To. Be. A. Good. Day.

But just as I approach the double doors to Meagan's office, I see that a tall, leather-jacket-clad figure behind me is headed in the same direction. A niggling feeling in my gut begins to form, but nope, I'm not even entertaining any negative thoughts. This is my big moment, and I won't let anyone ruin it. Especially not him. He's probably going to the bathroom, which is down the hallway. But as I walk closer, the footsteps don't get quieter like I thought they might... they get closer. I smell his cologne before I see him. It's his favourite one, the musky, heady scent he only wears for important meetings with senior writers and the producers. I remember he wore it at the Christmas party three years ago, when he pulled me aside and we, we... We had that really weird chat.

4

Suddenly Xander's shoulder brushes past mine and I tilt my head to peer up at him.

'Oh, hello, Yara, didn't see you down there.' Ugh, he's so patronising. His voice is deep. I can't quite explain it, but it's almost velvety with a slight rasp. It always manages to send a tingling feeling down my back – it's the irritation, I know.

'Hi, Xandy,' I throw back at him. *Xandy* – where'd I even get that from? As soon as the words escape my mouth, I immediately want to take them back. What a terrible response! I just know I'm going to be tossing and turning in bed tonight thinking of everything I could have said instead. *Is it hard to see us mere mortals from up on your high horse, you egotistical prick? Oh, you still work here? Timothée Chalamet hasn't returned your calls, I suppose.*

His lip begins to curl up, almost but not fully a smile. Those are reserved for very rare occasions.

'Did you miss me, Yazza Dazzler?'

'Trust me, Xander, there will never be a moment in my life where I will ever miss you... and you know it's Yara.'

When I first started here, my big sister Elif sent a huge bunch of flowers to my desk with a card that said, 'Congratulations on following your dreams. It's a long journey but I know you'll make it, Yazza Dazzler'. I was mortified, but what made it worse was Xander saw the note and started calling me by that stupid family nickname. Despite years of my protesting, somehow it's stuck.

'Sorry I must have missed the memo... Yazza.'

I let out an exasperated sigh and carried on walking. I hear an amused chuckle echo behind me. Honestly, this man is so infuriating. It's like he lives to get a rise out of me.

I breathe a sigh of relief when I realise he's no longer following me. I guess it was just like I thought. Bathroom, after all. I reach the double doors to Meagan's office, close my eyes and think to myself, *This is it. You've worked here three years. You've risen from coffee and lunch runs to being a real voice in the writers' room. You just need a chance to prove yourself, to get that top writing credit.* I enter Meagan's office. There are floor-to-ceiling windows offering an expansive view of the London cityscape. I can see right across from Battersea Power Station to the London Eye and the Shard. Perks of being the showrunner and an executive producer, I guess.

'Ah, Yara, thank you for meeting with me on such short notice.' Meagan looks immaculate, as always. There's not a hair out of place. From her brand-new Louboutins to the jumper tied round her shoulders, she's the epitome of stylish yet casual. My eyes take in her beautifully styled blond hair. If her fresh blowout is anything to go by, she uses her hefty hard-earned pay cheque on almost daily trips to the salon.

'No bother at all,' I respond, trying to keep the eagerness out of my voice.

'So, how was your weekend?' she asks. Her pale green eyes are gentle and the softness in her gaze puts me at ease.

It's what I admire so much about Meagan. She's kind and she really cares. In an industry full of cut-throat men out for themselves, she shows you can get to the top without losing sight of what really matters.

'It was great, thank you! I spent Saturday at the park with my friends, trying to make the most out of the weather before it goes all doom and gloom again. What a gorgeous autumn we're having! Thank goodness there were no incidents, although I did almost fall into the reservoir, wouldn't that have been a total disaster?' Meagan smiles but her eyes widen slightly. Ah, I'm doing what I always do when I'm nervous. Oversharing. Talking at a million miles an hour.

'And yours?' I manage to say before I let spill that I spent my Sunday forensically scrolling through Theo's girlfriend's Instagram. Meagan doesn't need to know about Claire's 7 a.m. Pilates class and iced blueberry matcha. Of course he's with someone called Claire. She's the very image of perfection with her sculpted abs and blemish-free complexion, and to top it all off she's called Claire. It's just so wonderfully *lovely*, isn't it? Not that I care. Not in the slightest. Everyone checks in on their exes from time to time. Even if it has been three years. I just like to keep an eye on him, like a Nintendog.

'Did you end up going to that new fancy restaurant with M...' I click my fingers as Meagan's new partner's name dances on the top of my tongue.

'Mike, wasn't it, Meagan?' a deep voice rumbles behind me.

Did I say I had a good feeling about today? Well, I am taking it back.

I have never swivelled round on my chair so fast in my life, because right there is my worst nightmare.

'Xander, what a wonderful surprise,' I say with such pleasantness I surprise myself.

He raises a dark eyebrow, looking impressed with my acting skills. If Meagan doesn't promote me, maybe I'll have a chance for some supporting role as a lady's maid or healer in *Claim to Power*.

'Ah, Xander, nice of you to join us, please take a seat.' She gestures to the one next to mine.

I'm sorry, did she just say... *join us*?! I keep my face composed, not wanting to show any hint of irritation. I don't dare to look next to me, as I can feel his gaze burning on my face. A million things are running through my mind. The first thing that pops up is the worst-case scenario: *Are we both getting fired?*

But then my thoughts spiral and I think, *What if it's worse than that*? But what is worse than getting fired? Maybe blacklisted from the industry, but then what have I done to deserve being blacklisted? Okay, sure, I'm not great at responding to emails quickly. And although I keep getting told characterisation is one of my strengths, I know my plotting could be better. A few of my suggestions have been rejected recently, but that's normal, right? It's all part of the writing process. But, of course, it's always *What a great point, Xander* and *Yes, mate, that really progresses the action.* Classic boys' club. Even with Meagan in charge, she can't change everything—

A throat clears and I realise that I was lost to my thoughts and must have spaced out. Meagan and Xander have been talking this whole time. About what? God, I don't even want to think about how my face looks right now. Especially in his presence. Why do I always embarrass myself like this when he is around? I've been staring blankly for a good couple of minutes. They seem to have come to some agreement. Xander looks delighted – good, not fired or blacklisted then. Meagan is smiling broadly, nodding at me.

My eyes dart around the room and I see two pairs of eyes looking at me expectantly. I let out a startled chuckle.

'Yes, so...' I start, hoping one of them takes the lead and carries on the conversation.

'This could be such an incredible opportunity – for both of you,' Meagan says with such joy in her face that I can't help but return an enthusiastic smile. 'So, what do you think of the idea?'

'Oh, right... The idea, which is *so* great by the way... I am one hundred per cent on board.'

'Yeah? I'm glad that you think this idea is *so* great,' Xander says, amused, tilting his head. I look into his eyes but there's an emotion I can't pinpoint. Almost smug? It's like he can see straight through my act. He folds over his Moleskine notebook and puts it in his back pocket, the pen behind his ear. Who does he think he is? Jack Kerouac?

'Yep, isn't that what I just said? I absolutely love it.' I know that I am probably doing too much, but I can just add it to the list of things I will lose sleep over tonight.

'Well, that's great news,' Meagan responds. 'I'm glad you think so because I'm not going to lie, I was a little worried. I know how you and Xander butt heads, but that's exactly why I need both of you on this.'

So we're working together on something. That's just brilliant. What is it? The cogs of my mind are turning at an alarming speed. *What have I just agreed to? Have I just sold my soul to the devil?*

I look to my right and I see Xander staring at me. I feel like he's rifling through my thoughts and I blush instinctively. He stands relaxed, hands in his pockets with his artfully scruffy band T-shirt and faded blue jeans, his eyebrow quirked. I hate how he can at the same time look so casual but also like he's just stepped out of a *GQ* magazine shoot. Between strands of his tousled black hair, I can see a glint in his eye. I'm really glad he is finding this funny, because amusement is the last thing I'm feeling right now.

'So, I'll leave you two to work things out between yourselves, but I trust you completely. Remember, I want to see what you've put together in six weeks' time.'

Six weeks? A month and a half to do what? I'm glad Meagan thinks that we can work together without ripping each other's heads off. It would help if I knew what she was talking about. But right now, the only thing I can do is smile and nod enthusiastically.

It is safe to say that this is not what I thought would happen when I walked into the office today. Somehow, instead of getting my dream promotion as lead screenwriter, I'm being forced to work with my arch-nemesis. And I don't even know what on. It could be anything. A tricky scene, maybe? Or are we to start an initiative to recycle coffee grounds?

'Well, this has been enlightening,' Xander says to wrap up the meeting. 'Thanks so much, Meagan.'

My nose flares at his tone. Whatever I've been roped into, why does it have to be with him?

Meagan claps her hands together with excitement. No matter what it is, I will just grin and bear it. I aspire to be like her one day and I'm sure that she's had to do her own fair share of questionable tasks. Maybe one of those included working with someone who annoys the living daylights out of her.

Xander has already stood up ready to leave and I rise from my seat to exit too. Surprisingly, he rushes ahead to open the door for me, and I can't help but be suspicious of his sudden show of chivalry.

'Thanks,' I say, begrudgingly.

'No problem, Yazza.' There he goes with that nickname. Xander chuckles and I feel myself getting redder by the second.

The minute we are out of earshot, I turn round and, as casually as I can, say, 'Hey, so what do you think about what Meagan said?'

'I have no idea what you're talking about,' he says. 'Or maybe I should say, you have no idea what Meagan was talking about?'

'What? I—' I can only defend myself in splutters. 'I just wanted to know what you thought!'

'Oh, Yara, I could tell from your face that you weren't listening to that entire meeting. What exactly were you thinking about, huh? Anything exciting?'

'I was totally listening and no, I wasn't thinking about anything exciting. Just thinking about this project,' I huff out.

'Right,' he replies. He doesn't correct me, so at least I know it is a project that we're to work on, as vague as that may be. 'It's okay, I know you're just too embarrassed to say you were thinking about me.'

'I'm sorry, could your ego get any bigger? Thinking about you? Why on earth would I ever think about you?'

Maybe it's the reflection of the light but I swear I see a flicker of disappointment.

There's something expectant in his gaze, but he shakes it off and chuckles. 'Because we're working together on this... obviously?'

My face is now flaming red. I need to find out what exactly I agreed to in that meeting and I can't straight up ask him. Then I'll have to admit he was right, and I wasn't listening and maybe, just maybe, I may have been thinking about him. But only thinking about his writing and whether we were both being blacklisted.

I'll find out one way or another. I spin on my heel and head towards my desk so I can begin to plan.

'I can't wait to work on this *project* with you, Xander, I'm sure it's going to be an absolute delight,' I throw over my shoulder.

'Looking forward to it, Yazza,' he yells back at me. As he walks away, I see that damn notebook peeking out of his jeans pocket.

Chapter Two

Screw him. I wish I could wipe that infuriating smirk right off his face! The meeting replays in my mind over and over again like something straight out of my nightmares. I'm back at my desk staring at the blank screen of my laptop as the cursor blinks tauntingly at me.

I peer over and see that Xander returned to his desk and is typing away furiously. He does this often, gets in his own world while working, completely shutting out everyone around him.

I find myself thinking about the day we met. It was my first day and I had just walked into the building, giddy with excitement. I couldn't believe my luck in landing a job working on one of the most successful shows on the planet. Before that I had only worked on short films and indie projects, so getting this job would be a big deal to anyone in the industry, but especially for someone like me who had no connections, basically no experience and just a whole lot of enthusiasm. I made my way to the reception desk, where I was informed that I was a couple of minutes early but that a 'Xander' would be down shortly to give me a tour of the building and show me the ropes.

I was waiting a while. Seconds turned into minutes of me trying to look busy, playing on my phone and staring at my lap. But I didn't let that bother me. This was a big show. The biggest. People were busy. After an hour of the receptionist throwing me pitying looks, probably thinking I was some deranged superfan hoping to meet one of the actors, this 'Xander' finally graced me with his presence. His tardiness should've been my first clue about the sort of person he is, but I've always been an optimist. When the elevator doors opened, and I saw an Adonis walking towards me, I had to pinch myself because I thought that no man was that good-looking in real life. Tall, broad-shouldered, with lightly golden skin and black hair that fell in perfect curls just slightly over his eyes. He also looked around my age, which I was pleasantly surprised by. Getting into the writers' room in a very junior role like mine was rare, especially on a huge show like *Claim to Power*, so to see a fellow young writer was a welcome sight. I thought we might become friends, maybe even more. Almost instantly, he ignited a crush in me. Nothing serious. But Theo and I had just broken up and it was a nice pick-me-up to have some eye-candy on my first day. I wish I could go back in time to snap some sense into myself for being so starstruck by him.

Thinking back now, I realise he looked slightly hungover that morning. Unfortunately, he's handsome enough to pull it off, but now I've worked for him for a few years I know his skin is usually unblemished by the dark circles he had that day and he was even moodier than normal. Of course, at the time I couldn't ask him for sure, but he had 100 per cent forgotten about me at reception. He then proceeded to give me a half-arsed tour of the building. I cringe to think how smitten I was back then, laughing too much when he showed me the ladies' loos and said, 'Maybe I'll see you in there some time.' Present-Me scolds my past self for being so naive thinking that maybe, just maybe, he could've been the Prince Charming to my story. I found out pretty quickly that he was actually the villain.

At least I know better now.

The day draws to an end and the office starts emptying out, and it isn't long before it's just me and Xander left. The days often end like this. The two of us working across from each other at our desks, our computers blaring blue light to keep us awake. But seeing as I have no idea what I should be working on, I've spent the whole day concocting a plan. A genius one, might I add. All I have to do is wait until Xander has left, which will give me the perfect opportunity to look in his notebook and find out what was discussed in that meeting. Then I'll be able to start work on this mysterious project. The sooner the better. We only have six weeks after all.

But it's almost 7 p.m. and Xander is still at his desk typing like there is no tomorrow. Gah! Why can't this man just go home? I have to up my game… maybe I can annoy him enough that he'll want to leave. I stretch out my arms and let out a big fake yawn, but I overdo it, because gravity fails me and I get flung backwards in my office chair. As I crash in a heap on the floor, I see my life flash before my eyes: Theo, Elif, Mum, Dad, my friends, the half-finished book on my bedside table, Xander. Why's he always just there?

I'm sprawled out gathering my senses when I hear the thump of footsteps running towards me.

'Yara! Hey, are you okay?' He crouches down, reaching for me.

If it weren't highly likely that I just inflicted a concussion on myself, I would think I hear concern in his voice. In fact, that's a good test. If I ever genuinely believe Xander cares for me, then I have most definitely sustained some sort of brain injury.

Xander is clicking his fingers in front of my eyes. 'Talk to me. How many fingers am I holding up?'

I stare at him dumbfoundedly. He can't seriously be worried… can he?

'Hmm, maybe four?' I reply, as two fingers dance before my eyes. Two deliciously large—NOPE. Not even going to finish that thought.

'Four? You see four? Right, that's it, I'm calling an ambulance.' He slaps his hands on his knees and makes a move to stand up.

'Don't be ridiculous, I know you're holding up three,' I reply, just to mess with him some more.

His body tenses and I stop it before it goes any further.

'Oh, relax, there are two. I'm fine!'

'That isn't funny, Yara, you could have been seriously hurt.'

He seems genuinely upset and I can't help a niggling feeling of guilt in my stomach.

'Look, I'm sorry, okay, it was just a fall, I didn't realise you cared that much.' I punch his shoulder playfully.

'Obviously I don't, but I was just doing the gentlemanly thing.'

'My apologies, Mr Woods,' I say, bowing and doing my best Lizzy Bennett impression.

Whatever warmth was in his eyes is gone and we're back to our usual dynamic. The unease is still there, settling heavy in my chest, but I try to push it aside.

'You should've seen yourself as you were falling. I wish I could've taken a picture of it and made it into a meme.' He lets out a belly laugh and my face burns hot. I do a double take because not only does this man practically never laugh, but, the one time he does, it's at the expense of me and my clumsiness.

'I'm surprised you even know what a meme is,' I throw

out. He stands over me where I'm still sprawled on the floor. I make a move to right myself, but a large hand appears in front of me. As if it's second nature, my hand naturally slides into his.

I'm surprised by how easily he lifts me up to my feet, but I shouldn't be really, judging by his toned arms. Which I definitely don't ogle from time to time… For someone who claims that social media is making everyone too image-conscious and superficial, he sure does work out *a lot*.

I need to get my plan back on track. 'So, were you about to head off?' I ask innocently.

'Why? You gonna miss me, Yazza?'

'No reason, just curious.'

'I was actually about to head out, but good job I didn't. Otherwise who would've come to your rescue? I'm pretty sure I just saved your life.'

'*Saved my life?*' I guffaw. I can't believe the audacity of this man! Saved my life, my arse.

'You're welcome,' he replies with a huff.

He strolls back to his desk, taking his sweet time. I sit back down and try to look busy until he leaves. Once he's packed everything, I see him place his notebook in his desk drawer. The same one that he was scribbling in this morning.

Jackpot! Exactly what I'm after. I type away mindlessly until I see the heels of his scuffed sneaker disappear towards the elevators. Hmm, that's kind of weird, he usually says some sort of farewell, a *Sayonara, sweetheart* or something similarly condescending. Without giving it too much thought, I push myself from my desk and stride towards Xander's desk.

I plop myself down in his chair and I'm hit with a waft of his signature cologne. I close my eyes and inhale deeply. For a second my mind flashes to earlier when I was on the floor and he was leaning over me with his hand waiting for me to grab it.

Suddenly, I hear a bang nearby. My eyes fly open and scan the room. My heart pounds in my chest. Maybe it's the building security doing their nightly routine checks. I continue in my pursuit for his notebook. My hand goes to the handle of his desk drawer and it slides open easily. Look at that. Maybe fate is on my side after all. I start to rummage through, trying to keep everything in place. I find what I'm looking for and start to lift my hand out...

'What are you doing?' a deep voice echoes.

I make a weird squawking noise and drop the notebook, which falls back in the drawer with a loud thud. My gaze slowly moves up the figure of my rival until it lands on his amused expression.

Logically I know I've been caught and should just tell the truth, but I can't stop the flow of nonsense that starts falling out of my mouth.

'Yes, about that... I—well... I seem to have lost my phone! Yes, that's it, I think you may have mistaken it for yours when you came over and "saved me" earlier.'

'And you thought that it, what? Fell in my drawer...?'

'Well, I couldn't see it on your desk so naturally the next place to check would be your drawer.' I manage a straight face but my heart is beating so fast it feels like it could explode.

'So, you want me to believe that somehow I took your phone thinking it was mine, then I put the spare phone in my drawer and left it in the office overnight?'

When he puts it like that, it's not as great as an excuse as I thought.

'Yep, exactly. See, you can be smart when you want to be, Xander.' I clap my hands together, then crane my head round as if I'm still searching. 'Oh, well, it seems like it's not here. I'll just head back over to my desk then.'

I start to get up but his response freezes me on the spot.

'I mean all of that would make perfect sense... Except for the fact that your phone is right here. On your desk.'

'Oh, would you look at that...' A delirious laugh leaves me. I can't bring myself to meet his eye. There's quiet between us for too long, the only sound the hum of the fluorescent lights above.

'Let me tell you what I think happened,' he says finally. 'I think that you weren't listening at this morning's meeting with Meagan. And for some reason, you thought the best course of action would be to sneak around – terribly, might I add – and take the answer from my notes.'

He hit the nail on the head. He might be the bane of my existence, but unfortunately he is one of the smartest people I know. If only he could understand the show's characters as astutely as he seems to understand me. Maybe then he could write some character development on his own one of these days.

I start to come up with an excuse, but I know it looks bad and there's no point in prolonging this torturous experience any longer.

'YES! Fine. You got me – congratulations! Would you like a medal?'

He nods towards the drawer. 'Take it out,' he demands in that deliciously deep voice of his and my mind starts wandering to other things. Much more sinful things. But then I remember who I'm talking to and I'm snapped straight out of that fantasy. He says it again: 'Go on, take it out.'

'W-what?' I sputter.

'The notebook. What else could I *possibly* be talking about?'

I feel a blush start to form but try to remain composed. I reach into the drawer for the notebook and flick through the blank pages until my gaze finally lands on one that has just a single sentence scrawled on it:

JUST ASK NEXT TIME, YAZZA DAZZLER

That blush I was trying to keep in check? Yeah, it's now bursting like fireworks on Bonfire Night across my cheeks.

He knows. And he knows that I know that he knows. This situation genuinely can't get any worse.

'Was I really that obvious?' I groan into the notebook and dare to look up at him.

'I mean considering you were trying to get me to leave so you could snoop around, yeah, I'd say you were being *slightly* obvious.' He cocks his head at me. 'Bearing in mind you're one of the best writers I know, you really should brush up on your acting skills.'

My ears perk up at that. 'I'm one of the best writers you know?' I say with slight disbelief.

'Did I say that?' He runs a hand through his hair, looking exasperated. 'Ah, it's late, I'm barely making sense.'

'Nope, I know what I heard and I will forever hold it against you.'

'Out of this whole situation, that's the one thing you pick up on... Seriously?' Xander scoffs.

I tilt my head and smile up at him.

We stare at each other for what feels like a small eternity but only a few seconds pass. He clears his throat and looks away first. Well, that was weird, but I won't think into it too much, otherwise my mind will start drifting into dangerous territory. Places that I've not been to in a long time. That crush I had on my first day was pretty fleeting in the grand scheme of things.

'Well…?' His voice trails off.

'Well, what?'

'If you want to play it like that, then fine. Guess I won't be needing to go through the meeting notes with you.' He starts to turn but I run up to him and latch on to his arm, which tenses under my touch.

I rip my hand away. 'Look, I'm sorry that I went through your things. It was an invasion of your privacy. I truly am sorry.'

His gaze softens but it's quickly replaced by a look of mischief. 'Apology not accepted. You're going to have to do a lot more than that to earn my forgiveness.'

'Thanks, Xander, I knew we could both be adults abo—' Wait. What did he just say? My sentence comes up short. 'Umm, I don't think I heard you properly.'

'Nope, you heard me perfectly, Yazza Dazzler. I'll decide when I forgive you. Until then I own you.'

'*I own you*,' I mock him. 'Do you think you're in some sort of Mafia romance?'

'Mafia… What?' He looks confused but it's all an act to keep up his pretentious persona. He knows exactly what I'm talking about. It's one of my favourite genres and he's definitely overheard me in the office talking about them before.

I squint my eyes at him. 'Never mind! Are we going to talk about what happened in that meeting?'

He walks over from the doorway and plops himself onto

his chair, then closes his eyes and sighs.

'Right yes, the meeting. I'll keep it nice and short. Meagan wants us to work *together* to write the season finale. Both our names on the episode. Not just writers' room credits at the end.'

My stomach does a somersault. This is everything I dreamed of. I'm going to write the season finale? I can barely believe it. I feel my face start to break out in an enormous grin, a yelp of excitement rising in my throat. I'm just starting to consider the implications – Xander will be complete a nightmare to work with *and* annoyingly I'll have to split the achievement with him – when he raises his pointer finger, stopping me in my tracks.

'*But*, whoever she thinks does a better job, she'll put their name first and give them the lead screenwriter credit. The season finale of *Claim to Power*, watched by twenty million people around the world…' He looks down at his lap, that wicked grin pulling at the corners of his lips. 'Written by Xander Woods – *with* Yara Aslan. You can see it, right?'

And all that rising energy comes crashing down.

What. The. Hell. He cannot be serious. This is the biggest moment of my career – everything I've ever pushed for. I don't just have to *work* with my rival, but I have to share the credit with him. Worse than that, he wants to fight me for top billing?

I bury my head in my hands. *How on earth are we going to make this work?*

Chapter Three

Six Weeks Left

When I get home to my tiny studio, the finale – and Xander – is all I can think about. That writer's credit was supposed to be mine and mine alone! I've put constant hours in after work to make sure that if an opportunity like this ever came about then it would be handed to me, because I would have earned it. I don't want to share. Do I sound like a petulant child right now? Yes. But what better way to deal with my frustration than to order Turkish takeaway and rewatch my favourite show. Me, my steaming hot lahmacun and mixed grill platter, with an episode of *The Vampire Diaries*. This is just what I need. To decompress and *think*.

In the years I've worked with Xander, it's not like we never had to collaborate, but it's just usually in a bigger group. We've never worked one-to-one before. I'm not sure how I'm feeling. Selfishly, I'm annoyed. However, I have to admit that from Meagan's perspective this is a genius move. He's always the logical, more practical one. Me? I bring the creative, romantic side to the storytelling. Put those things together and it should be a recipe for success… right? At least that's what I'm telling myself.

As I sit here on the cold floor of my bedroom, I feel homesick. I want my family around me to talk through this dilemma. While I adore living in the city, I hate being away from them. If I think about it too long, this large hole of loneliness opens up inside me and threatens to swallow me whole. But I won't let it. I can't. The second those thoughts start to creep in it's very easy to get lost in them and begin to think of the what-ifs of life. What if I never moved to London to pursue my dreams? What if I had stayed back home in Leeds with my family and… Theo?

When I first met Theo during my last year of university, I thought I'd hit the jackpot. Secretly, I always thought I'd meet the love of my life at uni, and apparently here he was, arriving at the eleventh hour. He was handsome and had the kindest smile. I'd never been in a proper relationship before and it was so fun – for a while. But he didn't understand my writing, and never read a book I recommended, let alone a word that I wrote. When I told him it was my dream to become a professional screenwriter, he laughed and, just like my parents, thought it was time I grew up and got a 'real' job. I suppose for him, a tech-head who wanted to change the world with computers, what I wanted seemed pretty trivial, but that didn't mean it hurt any less when he started seeing Claire behind my back.

I quickly shake that feeling of despair and I pick my phone up and scroll through TikTok to distract myself. I save a few reading recommendations from my favourite BookTokers. I'm desperate to read the new Ali Hazelwood. Then I open Instagram. Of course, the first picture that comes up is of Xander.

At first, I'm affronted. Xander proudly boasts that he's above all social media. But then I remember that his sister Eloise randomly followed me a few months ago. He has his arm round her, but he doesn't look his usual, all-too-at-ease self. There's an awkwardness in how they stand next to each other, almost like they're strangers. Call it curiosity but I go on her page and begin to flick through the posts, scanning Eloise's pictures of brunches and family get-togethers for another glance of Xander. Given how often she posts, there aren't as many of him as I would have thought.

I have to scroll down really far until I find some photos of skiing holidays in the Alps from when they were younger. All of the photos have an artificial grain on them, so the people look waxy and hazy. There's a photo of a teenage Xander with a dog filter over his face, a pair of skis hoisted over his shoulder. God, I would've killed for holidays like that growing up. Not that I'm not grateful for the holidays I did go on – I loved my family trips to Blackpool and Cornwall – but it was a huge treat so, whenever we went,

I made sure to savour every moment. I doubt Xander did the same.

Okay, maybe that's not fair. I didn't know him then. I admit I have a *slight* resentment towards Xander. I mean he literally had everything spoon-fed to him from the day he came into this world. He'd never admit it but I'm pretty sure that's how he got into the industry. He'll have known someone or his dad is probably best mates with the show's creators or something. I respect the hustle, but it's so unfair when most of us have to fight tooth and nail for a shot just because we don't know the right people. And if he's going to be a nepo baby, he could be a little less moody about it.

I can't help but think how completely different our backgrounds are. It was a miracle my mum, a stubborn Turkish woman, allowed me to study creative writing at university. When I broke the news that I would not be applying for law like she thought, it was like WW3 had broken out in my parents' living room.

'Mum, I know you wanted me to go for a more... traditional route. But I've decided to do creative writing.' I remember squinting my eyes to brace myself for their reaction. A heartbroken look engulfed my mum's face. That's when the shouting and hysterics began. My dad just agrees with anything Mum says – which is testament to their love, having been together for over thirty years – but sometimes I wish he'd just stick up for me. The only sane person left in the room was my older sister Elif.

'Give it a rest, Mum, she was born for this. You should read Yara's work, she's really talented.' Elif's words had warmed me, giving me some reassurance that I wasn't making the biggest mistake of my life. At that, Mum had started running after us with a wooden spoon around the house like we were five-year-olds again. She barely spoke to me in the months before I left for university. In the years since, my relationship with my parents has healed towards an almost happy equilibrium. They don't understand what I do, and aren't quiet about how they wish I would pursue something else, but they see that I can feed and house myself, so in that sense they're content. They just don't ask about my career and I put aside how much I wish they would.

Blinking away my thoughts, I quickly exit the app and dial my best friends for some serious TLC. I jump slightly at my unkempt image on the phone. My olive skin could definitely do with some sun – you don't get much of a tan staring at your laptop. My hazel eyes stare back at me as I brush strands of my curly hair from my face, trying to look more presentable. It rings for a few seconds before Maddie's face pops up on the screen. She's always the first person to arrive at any event and is one of the most organised people I know. When I first moved to the city, I didn't know a single person, which was only *slightly* soul-crushing. I quickly learned that making friends as an adult, especially in new places, can be extremely difficult.

I spent the first few weeks here lolling about while getting to know my new home and settling into the job. I spent my evenings doomscrolling and hatching plans on how to make friends that I never followed through on. Soon, I felt like I was going to rip my hair out from boredom.

That was, until one day I decided to go to a book club. I wasn't really expecting much, to be honest. I'd seen a video on BookTok about it being held at a big, fancy library in the City, and, even though it's not my usual vibe, I put my big girl pants on and decided to bite the bullet. I was a nervous, sweaty mess but I made sure to get there super early. The organisers had reserved this expansive room that looked like it belonged in a grand palace. I immediately fell in love with the place. I could imagine myself coming here and cosying up in the grey chair by the window to read my book. As my eyes swept across the room, my gaze settled on the large round table, which had only one other person sitting there. I tried to hide my surprise because I'd arrived an hour before the start time out of social awkwardness and my aforementioned complete lack of a social life. I knew I was weird, but what kind of complete weirdo would arrive even earlier than me? I attempted to hide my shock and put a smile on my face as I approached. The girl was also in her mid-twenties, with long auburn hair and a freckled face.

'Hi! I'm Maddie,' she said with such enthusiasm it was hard not to match her energy.

'Hey, I'm Yara,' I replied with slight apprehension. 'Are you here for the book club?'

'Oh, yes! I just got here really early, this is one of my favourite rooms in the whole building, so it's nice to get some alone time here before everyone else arrives.' It was then that I spotted the book lying on the table. *The Seven Year Slip*. Huh, she had good taste. From that point on we were really good friends, even best friends.

The second ping comes through and Amira's gorgeous face lights up the screen. I like to think that fate brought Amira and me together. And by fate, I mean my own clumsiness. It was a freezing winter's day shortly after I moved to the city when I'd stopped by Lunar Books. It's one of those amazing bookshops with a plump cat and a café. Although it looks tiny from the outside, that's deceiving. It's like the Tardis, cavernous on the inside. I had chai latte to heat me from the extremely cold weather outside. Unfortunately, I must have been too excited, because I turned round with my steaming mug and immediately bumped into a girl with dark skin and curly brown hair. The drink exploded between us. Before I even had a chance to process, this poor girl, my victim in fact, starts apologising profusely over and over again *to me*.

'Oh my God, I'm so sorry,' she said, running to go grab a bunch of napkins.

She rushed back over, having retrieved the napkins, and she attempted to dry the both of us. But these were the smallest napkins I'd ever seen and I didn't have the heart to tell her that these measly heart-shaped scraps were not going do anything to clean either of us.

'Please don't be sorry, it's totally my fault!' I said. Because yes, it was my fault.

'No, I should have been looking where I was going! Let me make it up to you, maybe you would let me buy you another drink?' she said, with such a sad expression on her face.

'No, no please, let me buy *you* a drink.'

'Okay.' She laughed. 'You get me, and I'll get you.'

We both turned round to the barista, who was watching this interaction with utter bewilderment. He took our orders – she ordered me another chai latte and I got her a vanilla iced latte. I try not to judge people, but ordering an ice latte in that icy winter weather is really strange behaviour. Who am I kidding? I was totally judging.

I turned to my new acquaintance.

'Thank you so much. You really didn't have to do this.'

'Honestly, it's no bother. I would have felt awful all day if I hadn't tried to do something to make it up to you! I'm Amira by the way. I wish we'd have met under better circumstances,' she said sheepishly.

From that point onwards we were the best of friends. Who knew that spilling a hot drink would be the foundation of such a beautiful friendship?

'So?' they both say simultaneously.

I texted them earlier with an SOS and their expectations are high.

'You'll never guess what happened at work,' I say with a dramatic flair.

'Does it have something to do with Xander by any chance, Yara?' Maddie says.

'Am I that predictable?' I respond. I don't think that I complain about him that much... do I?

'No, of course not. It was just... a wild guess?' Amira says unconvincingly.

But at the same time Maddie says, 'Yeah, you really are that predictable. What's he done now? Told you that *Love Actually* is overrated? Stolen one of your highlighters?'

'This time I have a seriously good reason for it. You know how Meagan was going to pick the lead writers for the season finale and I had a big meeting where I *thought* she was going to give it to me. Guess who came in and ruined it?'

'Well, we don't really have to guess because you just confirmed that it was Xander.'

'Thank you, Maddie, but for the sake of the story just play along, okay?' I roll my eyes. I explain the situation. That we're going to have to write together, and Xander being weird about whose name comes first. How this is all going to be a complete disaster and that the next few weeks of work are going to be hellish. That it will inevitably end up with Xander getting top billing, with me as footnote beneath his powerfully posh name. And my writing career, which my parents have been against from the start, won't have advanced in the slightest and I ought to just retrain as a lawyer like they keep suggesting I do.

'Okay, girl, you're totally valid in your feelings because you have been talking about this for months,' Amira says. I open my mouth to thank her for being so understanding but before I get a chance, she carries on, 'Although don't you think you're being a little dramatic…'

'Try and see it from Meagan's side as well. Xander is talented, isn't he?' Maddie continues, 'You've said that, so you can't deny it now. Don't you think this will be a really cool opportunity for both of you?'

'But it just sucks! I've been waiting for something like this for years. This was meant to be my chance to prove my parents wrong and for them to take me seriously,' I say with a sigh.

As much as I love them, I can't help thinking again that my mum and dad think that I'm wasting my life in choosing this career. Both my parents are the type who want their children to become one of three things: a solicitor, a doctor or an engineer. Especially my mum. I understand where she's coming from, considering our cultural background. Immigrant parents sacrifice everything for their children and they want to see that all of that struggle was worth something and it has to be presented to them in a way that makes sense for them. I barely admitted it to myself, but I'd started to think of the finale as my big chance to make them proud of me. I could show them my name at the start of the episode, 'Written by Yara Aslan'. This could have finally been the moment where they finally believe that I'm on the right path, even if it isn't the one they envisioned for me. But now my name, *their name*, could be stuck below Xander's.

'We know and that seriously sucks, but on the bright side of things this could really be a good thing!' says Maddie. 'Plus, he's super hot. There are worse things to be looking at while you're working.'

'Oh my God, stop! I can't even see him that way, he annoys me so much. Plus you know what he did at that party!'

'Sure, babe, but we all have eyes, and that was years ago. You seriously need to let that go.' Amira laughs. 'People can change when you get to know them.'

'Maybe give Xander a chance and he might end up surprising you?' Maddie says with a pointed look.

'Yeah, maybe...' I trail off. No matter what Amira thinks, people don't just change overnight. And over my dead body am I going to forget what happened that night three years ago...

Chapter Four

Five Weeks Left

I mull over my friends' words for the next few days: *Give Xander a chance and he might end up surprising you.* It's been a whole week since the meeting in Meagan's office and we've yet to properly sit down together. Although some calls and online meetings here and there mean that we're making progress. Albeit slowly. Our conversations have been vague brainstorming sessions, but we haven't written a single line of dialogue, let alone a scene. I've felt Xander avoiding me, which I'm almost glad of because I've been avoiding him too. I don't want to give him my best ideas. However, we need to really get a move on as the deadline is already approaching. One week gone, we only have five left.

It's 9 a.m. and I've just arrived at our office with my chai latte in hand. The building is grand. I mean what kind of multimillion-pound show wouldn't invest in a central location and panoramic views? I greet Patrick, today's doorman, with a 'Good morning, how was your weekend?'

He grunts in response. When I first started, I thought he didn't like me, but I quickly learned that he was like that with pretty much everyone. Well, everyone except for the devil himself…

Speaking of, I hear a voice behind me just as I reach the lift.

'Morning, Patrick!'

'Ah, good morning, sir, it's been a while,' he says with a smile. A smile! In the years that I've worked here Patrick has never smiled at me.

'It sure has. Hope Alice and Ben are keeping well?'

I let out an audible scoff at their interaction. Alice and Ben. Of course Xander managed to get the grumpiest person in the whole building to open up about his personal life. Like attracts like, I suppose. My heel clacks the floor impatiently as I wait for this lift. I look at my watch. God, what is taking so long? My prayers get answered when finally the lift dings with its arrival. I head in and let out a breath. I turn round and smile as the door starts to close without any sign of *him* approaching. That is until a giant hand pushes between the gap and the doors shudder to a stop. Internally, I let out a scream, *Can't I just have five minutes in the morning?* Having to make conversation with Xander before I've had my daily dose of caffeine is a big ask.

The lift door opens again and in steps Xander. He seems too tall for the small lift and I'm conscious of how close he is to me. His dark hair is slightly wet, as if he just showered and let it dry on his way here. His green eyes land on me and his eyebrow rises in his signature mocking manner.

'Problem?' I say.

'Good morning to you too,' he sing-songs.

The lift starts to go up. Why oh why do we have to be on the twenty-second floor of this building?

Silence starts to suffocate me. I may hate the guy but I hate silence much more, so I broach a safe topic of conversation.

'So, the finale, exciting stuff, huh?'

'Yeah, exciting is one word for it, although you won't be saying that when I get the credit,' he proclaims confidently.

'God, you can be such a dick sometimes.' I cringe as soon as the words come out of my mouth. He glances at me, looking a little surprised. We don't normally talk this early in the morning and it just slipped out. I think that may have been a little harsh. I look up at him, but he merely stares ahead, the corner of his lip quirked as if he's entertained by the whole conversation.

We finally arrive at our floor and I can't get out of there quick enough. Trust Xander to make me feel so flustered. I've embarrassed myself and probably committed some HR infringement before I've even sat down at my desk. I need to start making sure I have my morning chai latte well before

I need to talk to anyone.

I see Meagan hovering between mine and Xander's desks as if she's waiting for our arrival. I take a second to think about my choices right now. I could either go there and get grilled about our progress, which is pretty much nil at the moment. Or, and this is the option that I'm leaning towards, I make a run for it. I swerve in the other direction but Meagan spots me and calls out my name. I put on a big everything-is-totally-in-hand-please-don't-fire-me smile and head towards my desk.

'Oh, Yara darling, how lovely to see you!'

'*Meagannn*, hi, I wasn't expecting to see you until later.' One of the perks of being the boss is that she gets to come and go at any time she pleases, and usually that is after 10 a.m.

'I was just so eager to see how both you and Xander were doing. You know how much of a huge responsibility this is, not to mention a *big risk* for me to hand the season finale over to two junior writers. So, everything is going well I assume?'

Xander finally saunters over to our station. I let out a breath of relief because, if recent Xander-related events have proven anything, I can't be put on the spot and I definitely can't lie convincingly. But if there's one thing I can thank Xander's private education for, it's that he's really good at buttering people up and blagging about work he's barely done. Explains a lot about the political situation in the UK.

'Meagan, I didn't know we were meeting today?' he lets out with a laugh. No one else will have picked up on it but I sense a slight hint of worry. You can't work across from someone for three years and not notice when they're stressed.

'Xander! Just the person that I was looking for. So, how's the finale? Because if either of you aren't up to it, I'd rather you let me know now rather than later.' Her tone is stern. 'As you know, there are so many writers on this team that would kill for this opportunity. Not to mention some of your senior colleagues, who aren't best pleased I've given this over to you two.'

My cheeks redden with shame. Meagan's right. This is huge for both of us. The fact that we've spent a week avoiding each other, and haven't even put pen to paper yet, it's embarrassing. As well as completely unprofessional.

'Meagan, you worry too much. Yara and I are making great progress. In fact, we have a writing session scheduled in this afternoon, isn't that right?' He turns to look at me.

'Writing session, what ses—' I start but he elbows me. 'Right, yes! How could I forget?'

'Well, I'm glad to hear it. As always, if you need anything you'll find me in my office. I can't wait to see what you guys come back with.' On that note, she turns on her fancy Jimmy Choos and struts back to her office like the boss-ass bitch that she is.

Well, that could have gone much worse. I turn to look

at Xander with a sheepish smile, to find that he's glaring at me so hard, I worry my face may melt off. I know that I almost gave us both away, so I choose to stay quiet and accept whatever he is about to spew at me.

'You realise I was trying to save us back there,' he spits out.

'Right.'

'And you almost messed it up like you do with pretty much everything else.' He rubs his temples, then puts his hands on his hips, frustrated. 'I mean, can you even walk in a room without tripping over?'

Okay, I take it back, I can't stay silent. He didn't have to get personal. Sure, I'm a pretty clumsy person and normally I can laugh about it, but it hurts hearing him talk about me that way. Like I'm this stumbling disaster. Why does it hurt so much?

'Oh, and I suppose you've never fallen over in your life? You've probably been pushed around in a golden carriage since the day you were born.'

Xander huffs out a sigh. 'Look, it was fine. It all worked out in the end, no need to get your panties in a twist. But Meagan's right. We have to stop pussyfooting around each other. It would actually be good to get our heads together in person rather than online. We have to be working on this all day every day because I need this to go well – more than you can ever know.'

He needs this? Mr I've-Had-My-Life-Handed-To-Me

on a plate needs this? I doubt *his* parents are sending him brochures for law school, waiting for him to fail so they can tell him *I told you so* and that they always knew the creative industries were too risky, too elitist, not for people like us. He doesn't worry about making his rent. Everything will always be fine for him. With his film school education and industry contacts and his *beanie*, there's no way he won't make it. No, I need this more than *he* could ever know.

Lost in my thoughts, I realise I haven't said anything in a while. He lets out a loud sigh and scrubs his hand down his face with defeat. If I'm not mistaken his eyes dip briefly to my lips... but that might have just been my imagination.

Shaking myself out of my fury, I say, 'Okay, let's meet this afternoon like you told Meagan we would.'

'I can't actually do this afternoon because I have... somewhere to be, but I can meet after hours. Don't even pretend like you've got something else going on. I know you'll be here like you usually are.'

'Excuse me? The only reason why you know I'm always here is because you're always here with me.'

'Okay, so are you actually busy tonight? Or are you not a workaholic loser just like me? I'm disappointed, I thought we might finally have something in common.'

I splutter, 'Yes—I did, do have something on tonight. And I happen to have a vibrant, exciting life outside of work. But it's fine because it doesn't matter. The finale is too important. Today, I will cancel my plans' – that I didn't have

– 'and make sure that I am here after hours, not because I usually am' – I totally am – 'and not because I don't have a social life' – I have Maddie and Amira but beyond that my friends extend to the characters of *The Vampire Diaries* – 'but because I'm determined to make this work. And together, we're going to write the best season finale ever.'

'Fine,' he says.

'Fine,' I snap back.

'Good,' he retaliates.

'Good,' I emphasise. Because I don't want him to get the last word, I turn round and head towards the opposite corridor. Even though I'm now walking away from our desks and, as we both know, I have a lot to do.

I linger in that corridor for about five to ten minutes and then, to draw it out a bit longer, I go and make myself a cup of tea in the kitchen. As I'm waiting for it to brew, I stew over what just happened. I truly do not know what it is about Xander that drives me absolutely insane. Why does a guy like that have to be so devilishly handsome but so incredibly annoying at the same time? Okay, I have my resentments towards his upbringing. How he gets given every opportunity, but also how easily things come to him. Although Xander's reserved, when he does speak he is so good at talking, at smoothing things over, like he did with Meagan back there. And people, even Patrick downstairs, just like him. He's *graceful*, assured, whereas he's right about me – I am always tripping over, metaphorically and literally.

But I also hate how competitive he is with me, which makes me feel even more than I already do that I have to fight for my spot, any spot, in the team. Why can't we just work together on this? Just write something really brilliant, and leave it to Meagan to decide who did a 'better' job and gets top credit?

As I'm replaying the conversation that we just had, my brain snags on an interesting tidbit of information. Apparently, he has somewhere to be this afternoon. And he hasn't booked the afternoon off, which is quite suspicious. Maybe he's going on a lunch date? Not that I would care. Not at all. I grab my drink and head back over to my desk. I glance over at Xander's desk, and he looks as unbothered as ever.

Chapter Five

Five Weeks Left

The hours tick by and before I know it the office has cleared out until it's just me and Xander. Again. He had left the office around 2 p.m. and come back a couple of hours later looking slightly dishevelled, his hair ruffled as if a hand had been running through it constantly. My brain went back to the idea that he was on a date. Some afternoon delight potentially? God, what a pig! Could he not have waited until after hours or the weekend like a normal person would?

We've been working silently across from each other for hours. I'm so aware of him. His too-loud typing. His breathing, interrupted by the occasional sigh when a group email comes through. Slack notifications. Ping. Ping. Ping. Can't he mute his computer? He doesn't look in a hurry to ignite a conversation. Great. Guess it'll have to be me then.

'Did you have a nice afternoon?'

'Worried about me, Yazza Dazzler?' He turns on his chair and faces me.

'Ha! In your dreams!'

'So should we get the show on the road?' he says.

'100 per cent. I was born ready.'

He inclines his head towards me. His emerald eyes sparkle even under the office's unflattering overhead lighting. There's something gentle and coaxing in his voice as he says, 'Shall we do it on your desk or mine?'

My mind halts... He's not saying what I think he's—

'To work on, Yara... Which desk should we work on?'

I glance at his face, and he has that stupid smirk, which is probably the closest thing that I'll get to a smile tonight.

'Yes, the desk... I guess we can do it on yours!' I manage to cough out. I bow my head and try to hide my reddening face with some stray curls of hair. My brain catches up to what my sentence may sound like and I quickly say, 'To work on, obviously, like you said.'

I think I may have just managed to salvage the conversation. I really need to get my head out of the gutter and focus on this damn project.

My head is still down but I take a peek through the gaps in my hair to glance at Xander. Unfortunately, he looks as good as ever. He leans back on his chair and kicks his red trainers up onto his desk. How he managed to get his hair back to the way it usually looks from how messy it was earlier is beyond my comprehension. Maybe it just falls back perfectly within a few minutes, back to its natural, flawless order. That would be just typical. Self-consciously, I try to wrangle my ever-unruly curls.

I gather my things and head over to Xander's desk. Usually, these workspaces only have room for one chair, but you can probably just about manage to fit two. Although it's going be a very tight squeeze...

I'm not sure why neither of us suggested heading to the meeting room, which would be much more spacious. But seeing as I'm here now, I guess I'll just make myself comfy. I survey my surroundings, grab the nearest chair and take it back to the desk. We get started, and my shoulder brushes his. My skin instinctively prickles with electricity from being so close to him – that familiar irritation again. It's like my body just senses how much he aggravates me. I try to ignore it.

Over the next few hours, we make great progress and finally agree on a solid outline for the episode. But we keep butting heads over what will happen at the end. It needs to be big. Dramatic. Appeal to every viewer's emotions. My opinion is that Layla, the main character of the show and the fey queen, should finally reunite with Atticus, the morally grey lord of the underworld who everyone hates to love. In the last scene, they should kiss. Which is what the audience has been asking for since the start of the show six seasons ago. We know now that Layla and Atticus were childhood sweethearts but, separated by circumstance and their competing duties to their families, they've been forced into war. This season has raised the question of whether they could reconcile. This has been the slowest slow burn in all of TV history and I feel like this season is the one where we finally give the fans the resolution they've been craving.

But Xander is not on the same page as me. I've seen the guy's Letterboxd top four: *Scarface*, *2001: A Space Odyssey*, *Reservoir Dogs* and the 1990 *Othello* with Ian McKellen. The man loves a tragedy and that's exactly what he wants for the finale too.

'Yara, all I'm saying is that not everything has to end in a *happily ever after*.' We've been agonising over this for the past hour, and I'm about rip my hair out from frustration.

'I know that, but the last few seasons ended in heartbreak after heartbreak. Layla and Atticus have both lost friends, family in the war. The viewers have lost those characters too. I think it's time that we give people what they want. And what they want is a resolution to their favourite love story. It's the beating heart of the show.'

Even though this is a fantasy series, it's the romance subplot that has kept people watching – and kept our viewers increasing year on year. Ever since season one, when there were no plans to have Layla and Atticus end up together, people saw their chemistry on screen and their potential. It's those two characters that have got people talking about the show online, through forum threads, ships and fan edits. From that point onwards, it was our job to plant the seeds of a budding romance in each season that would slowly build up to a climax.

'You can't be that naive,' Xander says. 'Yes, they have an incredible chemistry together, but they would never last because love like that doesn't exist. This all-consuming romance that you're after is unrealistic and we'll lose momentum for future seasons the second they get together. They'll only ruin each other and I think it's better to set the standards now than to eventually break fans' hearts in the future.'

I gape at him. 'It's a show with dragons and fairies, but it's too unrealistic for two people in love to stay together? Of course, you of all people wouldn't believe in love. What would you know about it anyway?'

'Let's keep this professional, shall we?' His face hardens and his body tenses as he lets out a cold chuckle. I can't help but think I've overstepped and I want to snatch the words right back, but it's too late.

He coughs, shakes his head. 'Anyway, I still think we should go with my idea. Atticus is already an established villain. Yes, he has some good traits, hence why everyone ships him with Layla. It's what makes him so interesting. But at the end of the day, those traits could easily be corrupted, which is why him betraying her is the ultimate ending. Already enemies, fighting for different sides of the war. It makes more sense for the story.'

And what a tragic ending that would be. In theory, the idea is good. Great, even. Which is why he's the celebrated writer that he is. But I'm still set on the idea that a romantic ending would be a better fit, not to mention a more popular option with the audience.

All of a sudden, we're interrupted by a loud rumbling noise. I look around, trying to pinpoint where it came from. I'm slightly concerned because it sounds akin to a growling bear who's looking for his next meal. Are there bears in London? I have the urge to check the news for any recent escapes from Battersea Park Zoo. It isn't until I look at Xander that I realise he's staring intently... at me.

Oh no. I know what that really loud grumbly noise was. This cannot be happening. It wasn't a bear. It was my stomach. I look at the time and am shocked to see that it's past ten o'clock. We were so deep into brainstorming that somehow several hours have passed and we didn't even notice.

'When was the last time you ate?' Xander asks, his dark eyebrow quirked up. Another growl comes from my left side.

'Um, maybe a couple of hours ago,' I say. That's a total lie. In truth, I haven't eaten anything since lunch, but he's giving off this intense vibe that means I don't want to tell him the real answer.

'Don't lie to me,' he demands in a gruff voice. If I close my eyes and imagine the way he's talking right now in another setting, I feel like I'd be kind of into it. I shake my head. These intrusive thoughts about Xander have been happening more and more in the past week. I need to get back on the apps and go on a real date some time soon.

'Me lie to you? I would never do that,' I say innocently.

'Yara.'

'Fine! I haven't eaten in hours. I usually eat around seven, but we were making such good progress, and it was going so well that it just slipped my mind. Look, it's no biggie, I'll just eat when I get home... or maybe tomorrow morning actually, because it will be quite late when I get in—' I start to ramble, but I cut myself off when I realise that he's grabbed his phone and started to aggressively swipe his screen.

Bit rude, seeing as I was mid-sentence. But I'm used to his cold moods. It's silent for a few minutes and I wonder what he's doing. His dark brow is furrowed in concentration.

'Hello? I thought we were working on this together?'

'We are. But in order to do so you need to eat. I'm buying you dinner. Well, ordering it.'

'I told you I'm fine.'

'You're not fine. This is not fine. You should have let me know when you were starting to feel hungry!'

Once he's placed our food order, we quickly get back to work and continue to clash heads over the final scene. Forty minutes later, the food has finally arrived, and Xander heads down to reception to collect it. At this point I'm absolutely famished. If I was a Tamagotchi I would've died by now. Xander didn't even bother to ask what I wanted. Who even does that? What if I hate what he's chosen? Although at this point, I will pretty much eat anything.

Now that I have a moment's silence, I tilt my head up to the ceiling and take a deep breath. God, it's been a long day. I close my eyes and feel I could fall asleep right here on my desk chair. I soon get a whiff of something delicious and my eyes snap open. I imagine I look like one of those sniffer dogs at the airport. Xander comes strolling in with several bags in his hands. What could he have possibly ordered? Judging by the smell, maybe something with chicken... or beef! He holds his hand out to me, and I stare at it blankly. I must've taken too long because he reaches for my hand and starts dragging me to one of the empty meeting rooms.

My gaze flits across the table, where Xander is starting to unload a banquet of gorgeous-looking Korean food. I glance at the logo on the carrier bag and recognise it as being from the place round the corner from the office. Wow, he went kind of overboard. I quickly pull out a chair and take a seat when I see him staring at me expectantly.

'Eat,' he says gruffly.

He doesn't have to tell me twice. I start to absolutely devour everything on the table, having mislaid my ladylike manners somewhere around three hours ago. I start with the kimchijeon and make my way round the table inhaling everything in sight: tteokbokki, bibimbap, fried chicken, the whole lot. Xander juggles a plate between his hands like a ball and then holds it steady, starting to load it up generously with his own portion. We eat in silence, both of us wolfing down the mouthwatering sweet-salty-sour combination of the dishes. I slow down only once I start to feel full, and I become aware of my surroundings again. For a moment, I forgot that I wasn't alone. I purse my lips in embarrassment. I look at Xander, expecting him to be in a fit of laughter at my full Neanderthal hunter-gatherer transformation in the face of a spot of hunger and a plethora of Korean food. But instead he's looking at me with something like contentedness. I assess myself and realise I feel it too. It must be all the delicious food – for both of us. Any tension from earlier has now left his body, and he appears to be relaxed.

'So, you said that you *need this*, the finale,' I say, thinking about our conversation earlier. 'Why's that?'

Xander shrugs, and suddenly looks embarrassed about the remembered comment. 'I've been doing this on my own for a long time. Writing is kind of lonely and you spend a lot of the time wondering if you're actually any good at it.' He looks up and I nod my head encouragingly in agreement. I know the feeling. 'If I write an amazing series finale—'

'If *we* write an amazing series finale,' I correct.

'If *I* write an amazing series finale *and* get top credit, then I suppose I'll finally know for sure that I'm good enough.'

He stares ahead. I can see he's retreated into himself. There's something a little desperate about how he says it. There's a lack, a need in him that he feels like he has to fill. His head jerks up and he looks alarmed that I'm still here, listening to him. His cheeks have pinkened, like he's ashamed of having revealed too much.

'Plus,' he continues, his tone harsher and more guarded now, 'if I get this, I'll be able to write whatever I want next.'

'Exactly!' I say, excited that we share the same thought process. 'And what will that be for you?'

'I dunno.' He shrugs.

'Some auteur cinema with lots of moody shots that's about man's search for meaning?'

He smirks. 'Am I really that obvious?'

'Maybe.'

'And what about you? Is it going to be a sugary-sweet rom-com where they hate each other at the start, but eventually fall in love and everything is flowers and rainbows and starlight at the end?'

'You can't have rainbows and starlight in the same scene. Just imagine the viewer complaints, c'mon?' I say. But he's right. I have always dreamed of writing my own rom-com. 'Well, so what if that was what I had in mind?'

'Knew it,' he says.

'And what would be wrong with writing a rom-com?'

'Nothing,' he says. 'Just dousing the movie-watching public with yet more unrealistic expectations about romance. Because in all these movies, we never show the audience what happens after the credits roll. Because these things, love stories, they always, *always* end.'

'You can say I'm an optimist and naive and whatever else,' I say, 'but I just don't think that's true.'

'We can agree to disagree.'

For once, we have a truce. I look over at him sadly, wondering what led him to this place where he's given up on the possibility of closeness and lasting love. He sounds so *certain* that everything good must end. He presses his lips together and glances over at me. It's like he's looking for my approval. The atmosphere is charged, humming with something faint but undeniable.

'Well, that was amazing, thank you,' I murmur and lower my gaze, surveying what little is left of the meal. Korean food is one of my all-time favourites. How did he know about that? And now that I look at the plastic trays on the table, I realise they're all my favourite dishes too. Probably a lucky guess…

'Don't thank me for doing what anyone else would've done,' he quietly responds. There's a lot of people who wouldn't, but I don't mention it, seeing as we seem to have reached some sort of peace. For once, I don't want to bicker with him.

'Right.' I clear my throat and start to tidy the mess, largely caused by me. Until his large hands land on my arms, stopping any movement.

In a flash, he removes his hands as if the touch electrocuted him. 'Don't. I'll do it.' He empties the table in no time. He's almost frantic, not quite looking at me. There's an uncertain energy between us. I feel aware of how small the meeting room is. His body moving around mine. He did a kind thing and the goodness of it emanates throughout the room. Or maybe it's just the left-over hot food. I stand there in a daze, partly because I ate too much and am now entering the food coma stage. And partly because I'm unsure how to deal with this new, unfamiliar ground we're on.

'Maybe we should call it a night,' he says once he's finished clearing everything up and the room has returned to the way it was before.

'Yeah…' I say. 'Thank you for dinner.'

'Don't mention it.' His lips tease a smile. We awkwardly stand there for a few moments, neither of us sure what to say to each other. It's kind of ironic, two screenwriters who can't think of a single line of dialogue. I move away and exit the meeting room, his footsteps following mine. I gather my things and throw them in my bag.

'Yara,' Xander's voice calls out behind me as I'm heading towards the door. I turn round and I see him waving a phone. My phone, to be precise.

'You forgot this.' He runs up towards where I'm standing.

'Right, thanks, I wouldn't want to be caught rummaging around your drawer again for it,' I joke.

He's silent for a moment, before he bellows out a laugh, and I stare at him in wonder. I don't think I've ever heard him laugh like that before, like he actually means it, rather than the fake laughs he does at work for Meagan and the senior writers, flattering them.

I go to leave again and I hear his loud shout in parting.

'Don't think I've forgotten. You still owe me one, Yazza Dazzler.'

This time I don't turn round.

Chapter Six

Five Weeks Left

A couple of days have passed since that night in the office between me and Xander. Since then, our interactions have been few and far between. I don't really understand him. He's always been like this. Cold one moment, warm the next. Sometimes I wish I could go into his mind and see how he's feeling. Truly feeling. Not just this facade he puts on in front of others. I thought we were making real progress that night. We agreed on pretty much everything except for the damn ending. Yes, I'm a romantic, but is that so wrong? And if I can't have an all-consuming love story in real life, then the next best thing would be to create it in a fictional story for people to enjoy. I'm sitting at my desk polishing off the outline for the episode, while Xander does some research on past episodes to make sure we haven't made any continuity errors. Our fans are forensic. Dare I say, they know the show better than we do or even Meagan does. We need to make sure we get all the details right.

I'm lost in my own work when suddenly a plastic bag drops on my desk, making me jump. I glance up to see Xander already walking away from my desk. I glance down to the bag, looking around warily to see if anyone else would comment. They all seem to be focusing on their own work. Xander has sat back down at his desk with a matching plastic bag. I lean forward and inspect what's inside. The smell hits me first, an aroma of freshly baked bread with hints of dill. It's a smoked-salmon bagel with a thick layer of cream cheese, which is my favourite lunch. How did he know? First, he ordered my favourite Korean meal, and now this. I mean I know we've worked together for years but I don't think I've ever noticed what his go-to lunch is...

He doesn't even bother looking my way for the rest of the day and I can't figure out his game. Is this a way to soften me up so that he can steal the credit for our work together? Yeah, that must be it. I shake myself out. It's just a sandwich. I start to feel the strain of sitting at my desk for too long: back cramps, sore eyes... yeah, it's not fun. What better way to fix this than going to get a nice warm cup of tea? There's not much a good cuppa can't solve. I head over to the kitchen and have just grabbed my mug when Andrew, Xander's work bestie and the script editor, sidles up next to me.

'Hey, gorgeous,' he jokingly flirts. While Xander is reserved and intense, Andrew is the opposite in every way. How those two became friends is beyond me.

'Hi, pookie.' I flutter my eyelashes in response. Andrew and I have a thing where we pretend that we're an old married couple at work. We probably only get away with it because we're so firmly platonic. He's not a bad-looking guy, some may say he's very attractive, but he's too pretty for my liking. I prefer a guy who's a bit more rough round the edges, sort of like Xan—NOPE. Not even entertaining that thought. Working together is really messing with my head.

'Listen,' Andrew says, 'as you know, I've been working on the new house for a while now and it's finally ready, so I'm hosting a housewarming this weekend. Would love for my work wife to be there.'

'I'm sure Xander will make the time in his busy schedule,' I joke back.

'Very funny. But I can have a work wife and a work hubbie. This is the modern world, move with the times, Grandma. So, will you come?' he says, holding his hands like a prayer.

Andrew pooled all his savings to buy a real fixer-upper. He's been working on this house for almost a year, removing all the 1970s wallpaper and renovating the kitchen and bathroom himself. I'm truly excited for him but I know Xander is probably going to be there, and I don't enjoy dealing with his mood swings at work, so I certainly don't want them in my free time. 'I would love to, it's just—'

I don't get a chance to finish my sentence before he interrupts me. 'Look, I know you and Xander have this weird thing going on, but he's not even going to be there!'

'He's not?' I say, surprised that he'll be missing out on an occasion that I know means a lot to Andrew.

'Nope,' he pops out with a grin, emphasising the *p*. 'Says he has something else on that night.'

Probably another date, I think. That strange, sinking feeling again. He should be focusing on the finale, not his love life.

'Hello, earth to Yara.' Andrew waves his hand over my glazed eyes. I blink out of it. 'So, does this mean you're coming? You can even bring a plus one! Maybe Amira?' he says eagerly. Ever since he met Amira at my birthday party last year, he's been hung up on her. She's been in a relationship for years, which he knows, but he still pines after her. Honestly, I think Andrew would definitely be better than her shitbag of a boyfriend.

'Fine.' I sigh, giving in, and just like that, like a puppy who's just been handed a treat, he lets out his legendary smile, which works wonders on other women. Just not me. I can't help but match his happiness, and give him a shy smile back.

Without warning he pulls me in and hugs me tight. A throat clears behind me. I'm not sure what causes me to push Andrew off me as if I've just been caught in a compromising position. But as I turn round, I'm met with a tense Xander, who's wearing a thunderous expression.

'You're looking... cosy?' His words are light-hearted but it doesn't quite match his body language.

I peek a glance at Andrew, who is grinning like the Cheshire cat.

'Ah, Xander, didn't see you there, Yara was just telling me how she's coming to my housewarming this weekend. Kinda sucks you're not coming, man. You'll be missed. Don't worry though' – Andrew puts a friendly arm round me – 'Yara and I will make sure this housewarming is *fire*.'

In another world, I'd say that Xander looks jealous, but that's just ridiculous; why would he be? We despise each other. Or I thought we did until the other night.

'Great,' he says tersely.

'Okay,' Andrew says, looking uncomfortably between me and Xander. 'On that note, I'm going to go back to work, see you this weekend... babe.' He winks at me and saunters back to his desk. I can feel the heat of Xander's stare on the back of my head as I turn towards the kitchen counter. I fiddle with the tea bags and sugars, anything to keep my hands busy.

'I take it the dating pool has shrivelled up so much that you've had to resort to Andrew.' His harsh tone startles me a little.

He thinks I like Andrew? I try not to let the shock show in my face. He seems annoyed by it, but I can't think why. Maybe he thinks I'm getting distracted from the finale. I've thought the same thing about him and all his dates. But it could be anything. You never know with this guy. But maybe I can use this to my advantage.

'Hmm, he is a pretty nice guy, right? Exactly my type. I think we'd make a great couple.'

'I'm sure you would.' He lets out a humourless laugh.

'Well, spit it out, it's clear that there's something else you want to say.'

'I dunno, I just thought you'd go for a guy that's more…' He pauses as if carefully contemplating his next words. He looks thoughtfully away for a moment, then shakes his head, laughing. '*Arrogant.* Someone who can deal with a high-maintenance princess like yourself.'

'Excuse me?' I guffaw.

'You heard me loud and clear.'

'I am not high maintenance.'

'The fact that you refuse to speak a word to anyone before having your weird spicy latte speaks for itself.'

'Firstly, it's not weird, it's a deliciously cosy drink, which you would know if you would only accept my offer of making you one! Secondly, yes, I may not be a morning person but that doesn't make me high maintenance… I just like my sleep, that's all.'

'Right. You don't have to get defensive you know, there's

nothing wrong with being high maintenance.' Xander lets out a laugh. 'I don't mind it actually.'

'Why aren't you going to Andrew's party anyway? Surely you want to be there for your best mate? This is a big deal. Moving into a house that you've practically built from the ground up is no joke.'

Xander's eyes dart all over my face, but I'm not too sure what he's looking for. In the end, he pulls his signature smirk and replies with an infuriating, 'Wouldn't you like to know?'

Chapter Seven

Four Weeks Left

'Amira, don't do this to me,' I beg over the phone. Earlier in the week she had given me her word that she would come to Andrew's housewarming with me and now she's backing out.

'You know I wouldn't if I had another choice, it's just that Trent promised he'd stay home and look after the dog but he... you know how he is...' She releases a sigh. Yeah, a piece of trash is what he is, but every time Maddie or I bring it up it always ends in an argument. Why she stays with him is a mystery to me. He constantly does this, makes promises he can't keep. He's always either cancelling plans or never making them.

'Yeah, don't worry. It's fine. I get it, and there's no way you can leave sweet little Max all by himself! I would never forgive you.'

Max is their eight-year-old adopted golden lab and he

is the cutest thing to ever walk this earth. Sorry, actually, that was a lie. In fact, Max is incredibly ugly with one eye too big for the other and paws that are never clean, with his passion for muddy puddles. But I have a soft spot for animals who come from a bad home. Poor Max was just a baby when his previous owners left him for dead after neglecting him for weeks. It was a miracle he survived.

I know that if I hadn't reassured her she would've been racked with guilt, and, as much as I would have loved her to come with me, I can't do that to my best friend.

'Thanks, Yara! And have fun. Tell Andrew I said hi.'

'He'll love that. Okay, love you! I got to go.' I quickly wrap up the call. I was supposed to arrive twenty minutes ago but I'm still doing my hair. Sticking on lashes is not my forte and it takes me longer than I expected to try to get them to look even remotely similar. Before I set off, I take a long hard look at myself in the mirror, making sure everything is in place. My pink top contrasts nicely with my dark trousers, smart yet casual. I make sure I have every-thing, before throwing on a cute trench coat, grabbing the black Prada bag that I guiltily splurged on with my first writer's pay cheque and which I only take out for special occasions.

The Uber pulls up to Andrew's house just after eight. I step out and I look around the exterior of his new home. The place looks quite grand but still has an intimate, homely feel to it. As I make my way down the cobbled side street, the chatter of the guests clamouring from the back garden reaches my ears. I make it to the door, holding a state-of-the-art blender in my hands. Even if I find it dubious how friendly Xander and Andrew are, he's one of my closest friends at work and there's no way I was going to skimp out and give him a crappy gift.

I'm trying to balance everything in my hands when I feel my heel get stuck in one of the cobbles and the world goes sideways. I shut my eyes, bracing myself for the fall, because there is no point in me trying to save myself. This happens often enough for me to know that the best course of action is to just let what will be, be. In a surprising turn of events, instead of the cold hard ground I was expecting I'm met with the soft embrace of a... bear? My eyes fly open, only to find something much, much worse. Xander. I internally scream. What is he even doing here? I thought he was supposed to be on a date or something.

'How many times is that now that I've saved you from impending doom? Or rather, the perils of gravity? If you're not careful, you're going to end up owing me so much you're going to go bankrupt.'

I'm about to retort when the front door swings open and I see Andrew's grinning face.

'Yara, what time do you call this? I said seven o'clock. Sharp.' He sounds serious, but I know he's joking.

'Oh, behave, otherwise I won't give you this super amazing gift.'

'A gift? For me?' He perks up and puts a theatrical hand to his chest. 'You shouldn't have. Did I say no gifts? I meant to say no gifts, but maybe I forgot...'

I let out a laugh. His antics never fail to amuse me.

'I guess you're forgiven then.' He hauls me up the front steps and gives me the biggest bear hug known to man.

As soon as he releases me from his clutches I sneak a glance at Xander, who appears to be bemused, with an underlying look of... something I can't quite identify. Not envy, surely? Could it be longing maybe? Longing for what? Probably having more than one friend, I think.

'Xander, you made it! How did you manage to back out of—'

'Yep, how could I miss it.' He abruptly cuts Andrew off, with a pointed look. My eyes ping-pong back and forth between them. Judging from Andrew's puzzled look, there's something Xander doesn't want me to know, and Andrew can't understand why. Maybe Xander was with that girl again from the other week. Or even a new one – he's definitely that sort. At that thought, my stomach sours, but it's probably a bad lunch. I shouldn't keep trusting the food Xander buys me. Why Xander dating would be a secret beats me. Andrew's told me all about his conquests in the past.

'Right, shall we head in? Let me give you a mini tour of my *mojo dojo casa house*.'

Safe to say, this is why I can never even consider Andrew as a serious dating prospect. That, right there, was a major ick.

Xander's hand reaches out dangerously close to my lower back, but he must have thought better of it because he quickly snatches his hand away, avoiding eye contact with me.

We walk into the entrance, and I feel like I've just stepped into a luxury showroom.

'Wow, Andrew, I love it already, I honestly didn't know you had it in you.'

'You know me, Yara, babe, I'm a man of many talents.'

Xander looms behind me, his presence almost suffocating.

Andrew takes us around the rest of the house, which is beautiful. The place is tastefully decorated, with mid-century furniture and the walls painted in deep blues and greens. For the party, he's added some autumnal-themed pieces all over to go with the current season. Leaf-shaped coasters, auburn-coloured cushions. Everything goes really well. It's welcoming and put together, just like Andrew.

He finally leads us to the backyard, where I spot our work colleagues and some of his other friends who I've met before at Andrew's past birthday parties.

I head over, leaving Xander and Andrew to chat among themselves. I say hello to everyone and make idle chatter, settling into a comfortable conversation with the group.

As nervous as I was coming here by myself, I'm glad I did. It's nice to catch up with everyone outside the office. Time flies by and before I know it I find myself chatting with Gabriel, one of Andrew's childhood friends, and it's lovely. Flirty and different. He tells me that I look good. He's impressed when I say I'm a writer on the show. Since Theo, I haven't really let myself open up to anyone, in a romantic sense. I'd forgotten what it's like to just have fun getting to know a new person.

There's a dip in the conversation and Gabriel puts on a faux-serious voice, 'So, Yara, you come here often?'

'Hah, seriously?! Is that what you're going with?' I snort.

'C'mon, how else am I supposed to charm you, other than my wild good looks, of course?'

I take in his appearance: shaggy golden hair, with piercing blue eyes and a tanned complexion, scatters of freckles decorating his face. He's not my usual type but he is a breath of fresh air, and he just seems so... *nice*, which is exactly what I need. After everything that went down with Theo, and Xander blowing hot and cold all the time— wait, Xander? Why am I thinking about him right now...

'Checking me out so blatantly, should I take my chances and run now or...'

I punch him playfully in the shoulder and he laughs. 'I guess you can make a run for it now, or maybe wait until after our first date? You've not even heard me play "Wonderwall" yet.'

I look at him through my eyelashes and I see him soften. Damn. I am smooth, after all! I've been so out of the dating field and I have never asked anyone out before, but I'm all for trying new things. 'How about we grab a drink some time?'

His mouth stretches into a grin, a twinkle in his eye. 'A first date? A girl who asks the guy out first, that's rare. Well, m'lady, you beat me to it, so I have no choice but to accept your gracious offer.'

Gabriel takes my hand and kisses it, like a knight courting a beautiful maiden. Good-looking and a bit of a dork? I may have just hit the jackpot.

Out of nowhere a towering figure appears above me. I don't even need to look to know who it is. Why is this man always appearing out of nowhere?

'Yazza, hey, aren't you going to introduce me to your friend?' He nods to Gabriel. My eyes narrow. Given that Xander's Andrew best friend, I'm sure he will have met Gabriel at some point in the past, so what is he playing at?

'Really, man? I haven't changed that much since you last saw me, it's only been, what, a couple of months?' Gabriel laughs, taking the slight in his stride.

'Ah, Grant was it?' Xander clicks his fingers as if he's trying to remember, but I can see through this act. He knows full well that's not his name. Xander remembers everyone's names.

Gabriel merely lets out a smile, but I sense him tensing slightly.

'Xander, what a joker you are!' I exclaim to cut through

the awkwardness. 'Just ignore him, Gabe. He's just flustered because his girlfriend ditched him tonight.'

My rival scowls with a questioning gaze in his eyes. I didn't mean to let my suspicions slip about his plans tonight.

'No worries, darling, this isn't the first time. I'm used to his shenanigans.' Gabe wraps his arm round my shoulder and pulls me closer.

I swear Xander does a sharp intake of breath, but his face remains as stoic as ever.

'We need to talk. Urgently,' he says quickly.

I let out an awkward laugh, all too aware of Gabe's body pressing against mine. I try to convince myself that this is what I need but it just kind of feels... wrong. Too close, too soon. Gabe's probably already eying up another girl to spend the evening with. Gah! What is wrong with me? I let Theo walk all over me and now he's effectively ruined me for all future interactions with the opposite sex. I don't know when I'll be able to trust someone again that way.

Xander's hand reaches out to me as if to silently say, *Let's go*.

I don't spend too long thinking about what to do before the decision is made for me. Gabe releases me from his embrace and nudges me.

'It's okay. Go. Seems like it might be important. But fear not, m'lady. I, Gabriel, son of Arthur Williams, shall endeavour to arrange a time in the near future to organise our date.'

Oh boy, this is so cringe but why can't I help but feel a little giddy at his declaration?

Xander gently grabs my arm and pulls me up, still not having let go of my hand. Without a word, we walk through the crowd of people into the main house.

Chapter Eight

Four Weeks Left

Xander doesn't let me go until we get to the kitchen, his warm hand radiating in mine. There's no one in the room but us. The minute he releases my hand, its sudden absence feels unnatural, too empty.

'So, what's this *urgent* business you had to drag me in here for?' I demand.

After a beat he lets out a choked laugh that lightens the tension in the room. 'We need to talk work stuff.' He shrugs. *Work stuff?* Seriously? We're at a party for God's sake, surrounded by people having a good time. Can the man not take a break for one night? Not only that, but he also pulled me away from a really great conversation I was having with sweet Gabe.

I can tell that there's something Xander's not saying. He's trying to look relaxed, but I don't miss the way his knuckles are gripping the countertop, to the point where they're almost white. His smile, which doesn't quite reach his eyes, feels forced. I want to scream at him, and demand he answers my questions, but I know I'll get nothing if I push too hard.

His green eyes track my movement as I take a step back. 'Fine, let's talk *work stuff*,' I say.

He presses his lips together, runs a hand through his hair. In the dimly lit kitchen, the room feels like it's got smaller and the walls are closing in on us. The music, the chatter, everything surrounding us is a distant hum in the background and all I can focus on is Xander standing in front of me.

My eyes flick down to the can in his hand. He lifts it to his lips, only to realise that he hasn't even cracked it open yet. I suppress a small laugh that I try to brush off as a cough. His cheeks flush. It makes him look almost sweet, boyish. Out of the office, he seems not quite as certain of himself, unsure where to put his long limbs.

'So, are you gonna say something, or are we just going to stand here not making eye contact all night?'

He pauses and tugs at his earlobe. He looks distracted. 'I just wanted to talk about our writing schedule. We've got just over four weeks left and I thought we should distribute who's writing which scenes,' he says with some conviction, but still not enough to convince me. 'And I wanted to check in on how you're feeling. About us working together and everything.'

'You're serious?' My voice is laced with disbelief. 'You dragged me away from talking to a really nice guy to ask about *this*?'

'I know you weren't happy about it and I wanted to make sure you're alright. I can be competitive and stubborn and—'

'Arrogant.'

'That too.' He chuckles but it sounds hollow. 'But I guess I just want to ask how you're doing?'

'Okay, well, I think that this whole thing is stupid. Meagan is always talking about how important collaboration is and then she thrusts this weird competition on us? And it's not fair that Meagan threw us in this together, without anyone else as a buffer. No offence but it's not like we get on. I mean, most of the time I can't stand you,' I say hurriedly, the words coming out before I can stop them.

'Geez, tell me how you really feel.' His tone is light-hearted, but he looks hurt.

'Sorry, I… I didn't mean it like that. This is just how we are, how we talk to each other, right? I'm tired and stressed and I really just wanted to unwind tonight. And I really thought this opportunity was going to go to me, I needed it to—' I cut myself off, realising I've already said more than I wanted to. Xander doesn't need to know all about my family and my hopes and dreams. He'd probably only pity me and that's the last thing I need.

But Xander's looking at me with a curious glint in his eye. 'You needed it to...? To do what?'

I hesitate for a moment before taking a deep breath. 'To prove to my parents that this is more than a silly job before I get started on a real career.' The truth rolls off my tongue, my voice softer now.

'It's not a silly job,' Xander says. He bites his lip before he continues, 'And you're an incredible writer, so don't let anyone make you feel like you're less than, because you are anything but.' It sounds like he's speaking from his own experience, like it's a lesson he's trying to teach himself. Anger tightens his features, which warms my heart. A guy who has never pretended to like me gets defensive on my behalf and that somehow sends my hormones into overdrive. Wow, my standards are low.

'I know that. I do. And I'm so proud of what I've achieved so far, but it would mean a lot to me to just have them say *I'm proud of you*, you know.'

He nods like he understands, and maybe he does, maybe I judged him unfairly...

Standing here in the kitchen, like we've just revealed something to each other, it throws me back to that fateful night three years ago. I was a few weeks in, and I'd felt obliged to go to the Christmas party. My first interaction with Xander hadn't been great, to say the least, but I was all about giving second chances, especially since I had a crush on him. *Had*, not present tense. And Theo and

I had just broken up, so I was keen to get out there and meet new people. Since the trainwreck that was my first day, Xander had been making it up to me, teasing smiles, flirtatious banter, and I had felt something then. I would even have called him a friend. We had in-jokes, we went to grab coffees together, and gossiped after meetings. I suppose the way we spoke in those first few weeks isn't so different from how we act now – we were always having a go at each other, trying to provoke a reaction. But it was different then, warmer. I felt more sure we were on the same side.

For the party, I'd got all glammed up, wanting to make a good impression because all the cast and crew were going to be in attendance. I'd worn my favourite vintage Vera Wang dress, which I'd got for an absolute steal, that complements my figure like no other dress ever has.

As well as it being my first industry party, there was another reason why I wanted to look good that night. Xander had promised he'd be there and that I should *save a dance for him*. An hour went by, two, and there was no sign of him. I'd still had a good time getting to know everyone, but him standing me up felt like a punch to the gut. It wasn't until I was preparing to leave that he finally decided to show his face. When he stumbled in, he was nothing like the charmingly cocky, put-together guy I'd got to know over my first few weeks. His skin was ashen and his eyes were glassy. He was back to looking how he did that first day I'd met him. His eyes searched the room until they landed on me. Despite his unkempt appearance, my heart fluttered, and I smiled at him, but he didn't return it. I wish I'd just left then with my dignity intact rather than what happened after.

He made his way towards me, purpose in his stride. Luckily the room was still busy enough that nobody was really focusing on us.

He grabbed my arm and pulled me towards a secluded area. I remember it so clearly. I'd let out a laugh, thinking he was being a bit direct, but I was so attracted to him that I barely minded. Alone, he'd looked at me intently, holding me firm and strong in his grasp. Then, his lips crashed into mine with a fervour that felt powerful and sent blood rushing to my head. And I was more than happy to give in, my hands reaching for his hair and pulling slightly, which made him let out a low groan, his hands cupping my face. It had felt so urgent, so right, the friendship we'd been developing over my first couple of months bursting into what it was always meant to be.

The sound of glass shattering in the distance was enough to break the spell and he ripped himself away from me so fast, I didn't have time to grasp what was happening. He put both his hands to his face and rubbed them up and down. All he said was, 'This was a mistake.'

Then, he left, and we never spoke about it again. We never addressed the kiss and, maybe worse, we never got back to how we were those first few weeks. Friends. With the possibility of something more, maybe. But the next day in the office, it was like a wall was erected between us that I've never been able to take down. That's how we got to where we are now. Throwing sharp barbs the other's way, not worrying about how they'll land. Rivals who are desperately competing for the top spot. It hadn't always been like that.

I blink away my thoughts and pull myself back to the present. Xander looks at me questioningly and I was going to hold it in, I really was. But being here, in this quiet space, it takes me back.

'Was I really just a mistake to you?' I avoid his gaze. He doesn't say anything, but his brow furrows in surprise. 'All those years ago I mean…'

He looks torn and the silence stretches before us. I'm mortified, wishing I'd never said anything. What a loser he must think I am, still hung up on something that happened *years* ago.

'It wasn't,' he says quietly at last.

I look at him, the question clear in my eyes. *Then why did you say it was?*

But he says nothing, bites his lip again, looking confused and awkward. I cough, sigh, try to bring us back to whatever we can call normal. 'What about you?' I say brightly, too much cheer in my voice. 'Besides what you said the other night, why do you want this so much? You seem to have everything you could possibly want in life.'

He bristles, suddenly cold. 'What's is to you, Yara? It's not like it's any of your business. If you think I've had everything handed to me, why would you care?'

I shake my head. 'I *care* because you dragged me in here to talk about "work stuff", when obviously you want to talk about something else.' I take a step towards him so that we're only a breath away from each other. 'And maybe because, if we're going to have to work together for the next month, it would help to get to know you a bit better. It's pretty inconvenient for our writing schedule if you can brush me off whenever you want.'

I stand there waiting for him to say something, anything, that will make sense. He just stares back at me. 'Okay, you want to talk about work? Let's talk about work.' I try to keep the frustration out of my voice without much success. 'What's wrong with my romance plot? Why can't Layla and Atticus be together? Why do you hate love so much?'

'I don't *hate* love,' he says with a clipped tone. 'I just hate how it makes people – *characters* – lose control. It's like they forget who they are and what they want. And it's going to go wrong. Because it *always* does. Everyone ends up getting hurt and I can't deal with that. I don't *want* to.'

'That's it? That's the reason you don't believe in love, because… you think it makes people weak?'

He shrugs and lifts his chin higher. I can see him trying to reconstruct his assured persona, but he's given me a glimpse of what's underneath. I take another small step closer to him, so we're almost nose to nose. In another timeline, I'd close my eyes, and he'd lean down and press his lips to mine. In another timeline, he'd be willing to open up to me and I'd see a different side to him. But we're in the here and now, and our situation couldn't be more different from the scenarios I dream up in my hopelessly romantic head.

'You know' – my voice is quiet now – 'that sounds like a *you* problem. I don't know how you've been burned, but I can tell you have, so now you think everyone else is going to get burned as well. But maybe you've not experienced just how beautiful love can be. You're a coward, you know. You're afraid of what it means to let someone in.'

'I don't need love,' he mutters.

'Maybe not,' I say, not letting my eyes leave his. 'But maybe it's not about needing it but being willing to accept it when it comes. And not running from it just because you're afraid of what *might* happen.'

Xander glances at me through his lashes, still leaning heavily against the kitchen counter. 'Are we still talking about Layla and Atticus?'

'Who else would we be talking about?'

He shakes his head sadly before pushing himself off the counter. He leaves. Again. Just like he did at that party years ago...

Chapter Nine

Four Weeks Left

I skip into work with a spring in my step, humming softly. I've been feeling optimistic since the party. Okay, Xander did his usual hot-and-cold act, but I feel like we maybe made some progress. We had a bit of a heart-to-heart and maybe, just maybe, I'm starting to chip away at his walls. The past week of work has gone well. We've managed to sketch together drafts of the first few scenes of the finale. If we keep on like this, I feel like we might be able to work together after all. But despite my good mood, the moment I pass Frank, the other doorman, I feel the mood in the building shift. Something isn't right.

Frank avoids eye contact as I walk by. Huh. He's usually the friendliest one here. Like I said, weird vibes. A little confused, I shake it off, telling myself maybe he was just tired or something personal might have been going on. I make a note to ask him about it later. But as soon as I've made my way onto the twenty-second floor, and set foot in the office, I can't help but notice all the hushed whispers from my co-workers. The faint sounds of murmuring voices coming from behind their desks and the glances that people shoot in my direction.

I frown, and my cheery mood dwindles as I make my way to the desk. I feel eyes following my every move. Why is everyone looking at me like that?

I bump into Andrew mumbling something as he hurriedly walks away. 'Meagan was looking for you. It sounded important.' He's busy on his phone and doesn't stop – or is he avoiding me too?

As I approach my desk, I glance towards Xander's, which is notably empty. I look at the time. He's usually here by now.

I thought that we were on good terms since the party last weekend but, taking all things into consideration, could he possibly be avoiding me like everyone else? I feel a sliver of unease as I slide into my chair, ready for a productive morning. But the moment I sit down, Meagan appears at my desk with an expression I can't decipher.

'Yara. Could I have a quick word?' she says in a flat tone. Oh God. This is *not* good. I try to think of positive things, manifesting them into the universe.

I rush to keep up with her quick steps on the way to her office. Fired or promoted, that's the rule. Meagan's face continues to haunt me as we walk down the corridor.

Stern and maybe even a hint of disappointment? I try to rack my brain for any possibility of what this could be about, but my brain comes up empty. Xander and I have been working hard, making good progress. The finale is shaping up nicely. We have the outline and now we're just focusing on writing the scenes.

As soon as the door closes behind her, Meagan doesn't waste any time. She launches straight into the conversation like a tiger ready to pounce on its prey.

'I've heard the episode is going well?' She pauses like she's waiting for me to say something. She carries on, unfazed by my silence. 'I'm really pleased with the progress you two are making, especially Xander,' she says. 'He's really shown initiative with his ideas on the episode, and I have to say I'm impressed.'

My stomach tightens. *Xander?* It's *his* ideas that Meagan's impressed with? That isn't how it had happened. Not at all. We've been working *together* on this and, if anything, it's me who's come up with most of the storyline so far.

'He's really coming into his own with the character development, don't you think? I heard about how he's planning to resolve the Atticus and Layla plot. I love it! So romantic.'

Romantic! Xander? That must be my idea she's talking about. He's taking credit for my work. I open my mouth to respond but Megan continues, her voice having become more authoritative.

'However, I do think you need to up your game a little. I see a lot of myself in you, you know. You've been doing well, but it's clear that Xander's contributions have really driven the story forward. Yara, you might want to consider working more closely with him to make sure that you're both putting as much in. Someone needs to earn that top credit, don't they? Don't let him get it without a fight.'

My face heats in humiliation and embarrassment.

I can't believe he had the audacity to take credit for all the work so far. I had been putting in long hours, even longer than usual, and now Meagan is acting like Xander has done all the heavy lifting.

Meagan carries on, 'Actually...' she says with a smile that doesn't quite reach her eyes. 'I've been thinking about sending you two on a research trip to somewhere up in the mountains... You know, for you both to really get a feel for where the show is based, perhaps Snowdonia?'

She looks at me, waiting for a response, but I'm still too shocked to gather my words.

'I think it'll help you and Xander immerse yourselves in that kind of environment so you can bring back some fresh perspectives.'

My heart sinks. I have a feeling about where this is going. And it's not good.

Meagan tilts her head, a smile still on her face but it's now tinged with something I don't like. An almost imperceptible smugness, which doesn't really make sense.

'If you don't want to go, though, maybe I can just take you off the finale and call it a day. That way we don't need to worry about knotty, awkward things like whose name comes first – and who would be eligible for a promotion next year.' The words hit me like a ton of bricks. I can't turn this trip down. It would mean giving up the opportunity of a lifetime. Meagan isn't giving me a choice. Or at least, not a choice that's worth considering.

My eyes narrow. *Oh, what the hell.* I'm not going to let Xander ruin my career. 'No,' I snap, my voice sharper than I intended. 'I'll go! I'll go to Snowdonia. I'm willing to do whatever it takes for this.'

Meagan's smile grows and her eyes glint with satisfaction.

'Good,' she says. 'It's all arranged and you'll be leaving tomorrow morning. Saturday and Sunday. Sorry that it's the weekend, but all hands on deck, right? You'll be reimbursed for the overtime.'

'You've already booked the trip?' I don't even try to hide my disbelief. She knew that I was going to accept.

'Of course I did. I wouldn't be a good manager if I didn't. Time's ticking away and I want you two to get started right away! Only a month until I expect to see a draft on my desk, remember?' Meagan's expression remains cool and collected as ever.

My mind is spinning and I feel like I've been blindsided.

I don't know what makes me angrier, the fact that Xander betrayed me or the way I was so stupid as to believe there was a good guy under his cold exterior. He's exactly who I always believed him to be: arrogant, self-serving, unreliable. My jaw clenches and for a split second all I want to do is scream. But somehow, I manage to remain calm. From here on out, I'm going to do the best work I can so Meagan can't deny my contributions – and I'm going to make sure she knows my ideas are *mine*.

I force a smile and, with that, the conversation is over and I am dismissed.

As soon as I leave her office, my legs take me to my desk. I can feel my anger growing with each step. My blood is boiling so loudly, it drowns out the voice of the hushed whispers. Clearly word has got around that I'm apparently riding Xander's coattails and Meagan's had to have a word. I bet Xander spread that rumour too. I can't believe he's done this! The fact that he's taken credit for my hard work and deliberately made me look bad. I knew he was ambitious, but I had no idea he could be so cut-throat. I thought we were becoming a team.

At my desk, my mind races at a million miles per hour. But before I sit down my eye snags on Xander's station. He's finally turned up, and is staring at his screen without a care in the world.

I told myself I would be mature about this, but you know what? I'm not about to let this go. With a sharp intake of breath, I march over to his desk, and plant myself right in front of him, giving him a cold smile.

'Seriously? You went behind my back and spoke to Meagan without me. I can't believe I thought that, even for a second, I could trust you! After the other night at Andrew's and how well we've been working this week, I thought—' I stop myself and let out a laugh of disbelief. I want to kick myself for being so naive.

He stands up, looking bewildered, and I turn away, because I refuse to let him see a single tear fall down my face. I've always been a crier in arguments. Theo and I used to get into arguments where he would blame me for everything. I'd just crumble in a puddle of tears. I hate how fragile I was then, how fragile I still am, because I can still hear Theo's cruel laughs, even now. I quickly shake myself from the memories because I am not that girl any more. I don't want to look at Xander. I'll bet this has just made his day.

'Hope you've packed for our trip to Snowdonia,' I snap, making sure he can't miss the venom in my voice.

'What?' Xander replies.

'Yeah.' My smile widens. 'I'll text you the details. We leave tomorrow, so be ready to pick me up at eight.'

Before he can get his words out, I turn on my heel and walk away. I know if I had stood there a moment longer, I wouldn't have been able to contain the frustration bubbling up inside me. I can't believe he had the gall to look surprised. Acting like he hadn't just manipulated this entire situation to his advantage. He has stolen the credit for my good work and almost got me taken off the finale.

Xander has crossed a line and there is no way in hell I'm about to let him get away with it.

Chapter Ten

Three Weeks Left

My alarm blares at seven thirty. I barely slept after the whirlwind of last night. All I remember is calling Amira and Maddie in a panic. They dropped everything and rushed over and tried to make me feel better about the trip. Key word being *tried*. Despite them reminding me what a great opportunity it was and that it was only two days, I could still feel knots of tension in my stomach. The girls helped me pack, throwing clothes into my bag so quickly that I barely had time to see what was going in and what wasn't. Who knows if anything will match.

I can't believe Meagan was so adamant about me going on this trip with Xander! And not just any trip; it had to be to Snowdonia. The middle of nowhere. Hardly another soul for miles around. I googled it and I admit that it looks beautiful. In any other situation, I would be excited, but of course I'm dreading it because I have to go there with *him*. How we're going to stay in the same place without killing each other, or worse, is beyond me.

I look at the time. Seven forty-six: *shit*! Xander is going to be here in less than fifteen minutes. I jump out of bed, run to the bathroom and wash my face and brush my teeth in record time before rushing around to quickly do my morning skincare routine. Fine, yes, maybe he's right and I am slightly high maintenance. Sue me.

My phone starts to ring. I glance at the screen and see Xander's name pop up. With a sigh, I answer it, bracing myself for what I know is coming. 'What's up, Xandy?' I say sweetly.

'I'm outside.' Xander's deep voice comes through the line, sending tingles down my spine. 'Ready to go?'

I look down at myself, currently with one leg in my jeans and my make-up half done. 'Just putting my shoes on,' I lie.

Xander waits a few beats. 'Let me guess, you're currently half-dressed and nowhere near ready?' I can hear the knowing smirk in his voice.

I freeze. Of course, he can see straight through my lies, even on the phone. Sometimes I think he can read my mind. I hang up and go back to getting ready as quick as I can. It's a miracle I don't fall over from all the back-and-forth I'm doing.

I manage to pull myself together in the next ten minutes. I go for a basic outfit, jeans and a cute simple top. I put on my biggest winter coat and wrap a chunky scarf round my neck. I grab my make-up bag quickly and do some finishing touches, swiping on some mascara and a layer of lip gloss. I take a glance in the mirror and give myself a quick pep talk for the weekend ahead. 'You've got this, Yara. No man is going to tear you down. Never again.'

I let the words settle in my chest before grabbing my overnight bag and heading straight out the door, leaving the chaos and mess behind. As soon as I step out, I feel the crisp morning air. I glance around, searching for Xander in the cars lining the street. When I finally spot him, I do a double-take. A sleek, black sports car is parked right in front of my house. I'm going to have to ask HR if we're really on the same salary. It stands out like a sore thumb in my area that estate agents have been calling 'up-and-coming' for the past twenty years. I'd always known he had money but seeing him with a car like that makes me think I underestimated.

As I approach, I can't help but take a good long look at the beauty of a car in front of me. Damn him. Handsome and rich. God, what a deadly combination.

Just as I reach for the door handle, I hear footsteps pounding on the pavement, coming towards me. I lift my gaze to see Xander's towering figure moving to my side of the car with steely determination. He opens the passenger door for me, looking down at me.

'After you, m'lady,' he says with a mocking expression.

My eyes widen. I know full well he's referencing that night at Andrew's with Gabe. I try to keep my embarrassment at bay and shoot him a look of complete indifference. I'm reminded that I haven't heard from him – probably Xander put him off me. Another thing he's sabotaged for me.

'You think you're funny, huh?'

'What? I heard you like that sort of thing.' He raises his hands in pretend defence.

My face turns beet-red the moment I sit in the car. It's only been a few minutes, and I already feel a little flustered by his teasing. I want to scream in annoyance because he knows exactly which buttons to press to get a reaction from me. So instead of giving him what he wants, I just grit my teeth and throw him an unimpressed look.

Xander chuckles as he goes to the driver's side and slides into his seat, looking way too confident for my liking. I keep my gaze firmly forward, but I catch a glimpse of him through my peripheral vision as he adjusts his seat. I don't miss the way the muscles in his arms flex underneath his deep purple shirt, which complements his golden complexion. How does he have a tan even in the autumn? He's too attractive for his own good. It makes my blood boil. Not because I like him… obviously. It's because he knows he's so good-looking. His cocky attitude doesn't help anything.

He starts the engine, and a low rumbling sound fills the car. I feel that familiar tension building again. I am angry, frustrated and annoyed with him all at once, which isn't exactly how I wanted to start my Saturday morning. I have to stop letting him get in my head. I just need to write an amazing finale and everything else – promotions, solo opportunities, commissioned writing gigs – will fall into place. Then, I can forget about Xander Woods for ever.

Xander's voice breaks the silence. 'You're late.'

'I know.'

'I guess I shouldn't be surprised.' He glances at me from the corner of his eye, his tone teasing.

'That's rich coming from you. Don't you remember my first day?'

His eyes fall to his lap and – is that a blush I see stretching across those perfectly sculpted cheekbones?

'What's your point, Xander? You upset because I didn't fall in line with your little schedule?' My lips twist into a sarcastic smile.

'Always the rebel, Yazza,' he says, the corner of his lips quirking up.

I feel an unexpected shiver run through me at the comment. Gah! I normally hate him calling me by my family nickname, but recently it's felt different somehow. Makes me feel at home. I'm probably just getting used to it. Isn't it called immersion therapy? That's how they cure allergies and phobias, I think. I quickly push the thought aside and turn my attention back onto the road.

He peels away from the house, leaving my safe space behind, and we head toward the edge of the city. The car is filled with the sounds of passing traffic, urgent horns and road rage, until we finally escape onto the wide expanse of the motorway. Quiet. Too much quiet.

I ask Xander if I can put some music on, but he says he hasn't got any on his phone. Of course he doesn't. He mentions that there might a Bob Dylan CD – obviously – and I rummage around looking for it but can't find it anywhere. Xander says he must have misplaced it, but he thinks that the quiet is nice. I hate the silence but here I am. Stuck in a car with my number one enemy with nothing but the sound of tyres on the road to fill the air.

'Well.' He taps his fingers on the steering wheel. 'Wanna play a game instead?'

'A game?'

'Yeah, you know, a game, which is an activity that one engages in for fun?'

'I know what a game is,' I say with a deadpan look. I know I need to bring up the whole 'taking credit for my ideas' thing eventually, but not yet. We have a long journey and weekend ahead of us, so we might as well get along until the time is right. 'Which game?'

'Two truths and a lie. You know it?'

'I know it.' Why not? We're going to be stuck in this car for hours, and I guess it could be fun. 'Fine, let's play, but I hope you don't expect me to go easy on you.'

'You? Go easy on me? Can't imagine it. I wouldn't dream of it. Okay… you go first.'

I mull it over for a moment. 'Alright. I've travelled to five different continents. I hate spiders. And I once swam with sharks.'

'Swam with sharks, huh? Well, I know you're afraid of horror movies, heights and the dark – most things basically,' he says. 'Swimming with sharks, on the other hand, that seems pretty bold. Not something you would do. So, I'm going to guess that's the lie.' Xander studies me for a second before relaxing back in his seat. 'Am I right or am I right?'

'*WRONG*. I did actually swim with sharks when they took us to the Bahamas last season. Remember, the mermaids subplot? The lie is the spider one. I actually think they're really cute.' I laugh with victory. I knew that would catch him out.

'You think spiders are cute?' Xander stares at me in shock with his mouth slightly agape.

'I know, I know. It's kinda weird, but I saw this poem about spiders on TikTok once and it changed how I view them from that point onwards,' I say with a shrug. 'They're actually really misunderstood.'

As though talking to himself, he says quietly, 'I *hate* spiders…'

'You *hate* spiders? I thought you said that if you can't handle Tarantino at his goriest then you can't handle him at his best. Or that fear always lies at the heart of great character? But you're afraid of an incy, wincy spider?'

'Hey, I thought you liked your male characters to be sensitive and multifaceted? I'm showing a bit of weakness, here, and you're laughing at me.'

'Maybe that just applies to fictional characters. A book boyfriend will never let you down.'

'You're something else, you know that?' Xander chuckles and shakes his head. It does something to me that I can't explain. I have to remind myself what he did just days ago.

'Okay,' I say. 'Your turn.'

He nods thoughtfully, considering his words. 'Okay, let me think. Right, got some. I've never been on a boat. I can't ride a bike. My favourite snack is…'

We play several rounds and with every one we get to know each other more. Xander eases into the drive and is surprisingly easy to talk to now. We slip into a rhythm, finding ourselves telling stories we've never shared with anyone. I open up about how lonely I can find the city but how my friendship with Maddie and Amira has helped me through that. And even though they're always there for me, sometimes I think I need *more*. More experiences. More *something*. I talk about my parents, their impossible expectations, how they hate my career and I sometimes think they're just waiting for me to fail. Although Elif supports me, it's easier for her. She's a doctor and has a husband and a baby on the way and all the things that mean my parents think her life is good and meaningful. They're all things that make me feel vulnerable, but it's freeing, like a weight coming off my chest.

I can see the same thing happening with him. He reveals his family life and how, when his parents separated, he basically got shipped off to boarding school and no one checked up on him. How he has a sister – I pretend not to know that from Instagram – who he basically never got to speak to from ages eleven to eighteen, and he still feels the distance of those separated years now. He opens up about how he was bullied by the other boys because he liked books and films, not rugby and cricket. He says that – would you believe – he was a late bloomer and in fact pretty ugly until he was eighteen. Only then did he get handsome.

'So you think you're handsome?' I say.

'Well,' he demurs, 'some have said that it's true.'

I learn Xander barely speaks to either of his parents and they don't understand his workaholic nature. My view of him changes and for the first time Xander doesn't sound like the cocky, arrogant rich guy I've known for years. He just sounds… human. Maybe he's not the devil incarnate, but a person with insecurities and failures and a history like everyone else. *Who'd have thought?* I chastise myself.

'I'm sorry, by the way, about your first day at work,' he says.

'Huh?'

'When I was late.'

'Oh, sorry, I was just kidding about that earlier. I know you were hungover. It happens to the best of—'

'You thought I was hungover?' He laughs. 'No wonder we've been at war for three years. I'm really bad at first impressions, aren't I?'

'Of all your strengths, I'd put storyboarding and obscure movie knowledge at the top, but first impressions maybe not...'

He chuckles, one hand holding the steering wheel, the other resting on his thigh. He glances at me, then back to the road. 'No, I remember that day actually. My grandma' – his voice breaks, but he turns it into a cough – 'she was diagnosed with Alzheimer's your first week, although she'd been ill for a really long time before that. I suppose I was coming to terms with the diagnosis, but it's not an excuse, I know.'

'Ah, Xander, I'm sorry. You don't need to explain yourself to me.'

He nods, his eyes laser-focused on the road. 'It's also why at that party I'd said that what happened between us was—' He swallows, the regret clear in his expression. 'Anyway, I remember that was a pretty rough night for me, I'd spent hours looking for her because the carer had forgotten to lock the door and she'd got out with no one knowing where she went. I've never been good at apologies, but I realise I never said sorry for what happened. You aren't a mistake. You never were.'

His words fill me with understanding. Yes, what he said that night was hurtful, but it was his own pain that caused him to lash out at those around him. My heart aches for what he was going through. From what little he's said of his family on the drive so far, it sounds like he was pretty isolated, with no one to comfort him.

At my silence, Xander carries on, 'She only passed away a few weeks ago, actually.'

'Oh.' I glance down at my lap. 'I'm sorry. Were you close?'

'Yeah.' He presses his lips together, staring ahead. 'Very. But in some ways, it's brought my family closer. Not my parents, but parts of my family. Which has been nice…'

He looks thoughtful. There's a delicate trust in the car now and I don't want to interrupt it, so I stay quiet.

Suddenly, he laughs again. 'In fairness, I probably was hungover that morning too. Drowning my sorrows and all that.'

I laugh and let him know that, given the circumstances, he's forgiven.

Before we know it, the hills of Snowdonia are stretching out before us. I gasp at the sight. Lush, green mountains that clamber higher and higher so that their peaks are hidden in the clouds. The game has brought us closer than either of us had expected. It hits me that the rest of the trip might be different, better even, the realisation dousing me like cold water. We might see each other in a different light. Not work rivals or whatever we were at those disastrous parties, just people. A boy and a girl. Maybe, just maybe, this trip won't be as terrible as I had thought.

Chapter Eleven

Three Weeks Left

The sound of my hand banging on the check-in desk echoes throughout the lobby. The receptionist glances at me with disdain evident all over his face.

'What do you mean there's only one room left?' I demand, trying to stay level-headed. 'Our boss booked this trip, or the production company did. We're from the show *Claim to Power*, do you know it?'

'I love that show!' The receptionist lights up. 'Do you know they film bits of it around here?'

I grit my teeth. 'Yes, I know that. Like I said, we're from the show, we're writers on it. Is there really nothing you can do?'

'I'm sorry, miss. We're all booked up.'

I take a look at Xander and of course his expression doesn't give anything away. I wonder what thoughts are running through his mind right now. Is he dreading it as much as I am? Although if I look close enough, is that a twinkle of excitement in his eyes? Could he possibly be pleased at this situation? Great, he must be revelling in how awkward I feel right now.

'Fine,' I say and quickly turn to Xander. 'We don't have to stay here, right? I mean, we're in Snowdonia. It's huge. A massive tourist spot. There's got to be a million other places nearby... right?' Although now I think about it, I feel like we only passed campsites and the very occasional bed and breakfast on the way up here. But I'll stay in a tent if I have to. I am refusing to even consider the possibility of staying in the same room as Xander.

'Feel free to leave, miss, if it is not up to your standards,' the receptionist says. I see from his 'Hello! I'm happy to help' badge that his name is Tom.

My eyes catch with Xander's as he peers down at me. I can see the wheels in his brain turning. He's plotting something. Whatever it is, I know I'm not going to like it.

He looks like he's made up his mind, and lets out a huge smile, showing off those perfect pearly whites. My eyes flick back and forth between him and the receptionist as I feel his huge, heavy arm curl round my shoulders, pulling me closer to him.

'Yeah, don't listen to her, Tom, my girlfriend here can be such a *joker*, we'll take the room. Sorry, we just had a bit of an argument on the way up. You know how it is. This one gets such *terrible* road rage.' He lets out an easy laugh. All the while I can feel the heat of his body pressing up against mine.

'What are you doing?' I hiss through clenched teeth, but Xander keeps on smiling at Tom.

'Great,' Tom says, and he turns to his computer to finalise the details of our booking.

I try to break out of Xander's hold but he just pulls me closer, which I didn't think was actually possible. At the abrupt movement, my hand lands on his chest to steady myself, only to find his muscles bunching under my touch.

'Just play along,' he whispers.

I let out a strangled laugh, and I must sound like a dying hyena because Tom pauses his aggressive typing and gives me a questioning look.

Xander leans down to whisper in my ear, his scruffy 5 o'clock shadow lightly tickling my face, 'Go get some snacks from the vending machine over there while I deal with the situation.'

His grip loosens and he gently pushes me away. God, this man has no manners.

I start surveying the snacks available. The selection is quite sparse. Twix? No. KitKat? Gross. My eyes zero on my favourite chocolate bar, a Snickers. The peanuty chocolatey goodness is just too much to pass up. I was going to leave it there, but the last Twirl catches my eye and I know, from our game earlier, that it's Xander's favourite. I buy the Twirl too and lean down to grab the goods as Xander appears beside me with a pair of keys, shaking them triumphantly in his hand. I quickly conceal the Twirl in my bag, a plan forming in my mind.

'Got the keys, Yazza Dazzler.' He dangles them in front of me.

'Sorry, they ran out of your favourites, Xandy,' I say with fake sadness. His eye twitches and he presents his palm expectantly. I place my Snickers in his hand. As long as I've known Xander, he's absolutely despised anything with peanuts.

'Oh, how… delightful.' He looks a little disappointed as he says, 'I thought you knew, but I'm not the biggest peanut fan. Thanks for it anyway, but I'll pass.'

At this I whip out the Twirl, dangling it in front of his face. 'It's a good job I got this as a backup.'

'Haha. Very funny,' he says, snatching it out of my hand.

He pockets the Twirl and looks at me expectantly. 'Shall we go up and see our room then? I managed to score us their most expensive one, with a panoramic view of the mountains.'

'I thought they didn't have any spare rooms available?' I squint my eyes suspiciously.

'Right. They didn't, did they? Uh… they moved some other people around and gave us a free upgrade to apologise for the inconvenience.' Something about this story smells fishy but I'm too exhausted from the journey to question it further. I suddenly remember that we still have a bloody mountain to hike, although apparently there's this really nice pub at the top. Meagan has given us a punishing itinerary to 'get the creative juices flowing'.

'Uh-huh.' I nod at him suspiciously. 'I just want to point out I can't think of anything worse than having to share a room with you.' I emphasise each word so he gets the hint, but I can feel my resolve slowly slipping as the tiredness from the journey starts to sweep in.

'Right.' He smirks, a twinkle in his eye.

With that Xander gets close to me and places his hand on the small of my back to urge me forward.

'You ready to head up?' His green eyes pierce mine, and for a moment I'm lost in them, distracted by the feel of his hand.

'Ye-yeah!' Hopefully he didn't notice my stutter as I try to put as much cheeriness in my voice as I can.

His hand tenses, sending a tingle of desire through me. He takes a breath before removing it. 'Let's go then!'

He claps his hands together.

Chapter Twelve

Three Weeks Left

After what felt like a torturously long car journey, I can't believe we have to go up the mountain. I've just finished freshening up in the luxurious bathroom when a deep voice forces me to look up.

'About time,' Xander says, throwing a look at me from the chair where he's sitting pulling on his hiking boots.

'I'm not the one who made us late, with that little stunt you pulled back at reception.' I roll my eyes. 'I hate exercise so much. This is literally my worst nightmare.'

I groan into my hands. It's not like I haven't tried to be active; it just is never a good time for me, and I have accepted my fate of forever being a couch potato. And for someone as clumsy as me, I would personally class it as a health and safety concern. I doubt Meagan has submitted the necessary risk assessment form to HR for this trip.

'Yeah, I figured,' he replies. 'But you'll be fine. You won't die from a little walk. Plus, I won't let anything happen to you.'

My silly heart jumps at that proclamation, although I'm sure he is just saying it as a passing comment.

We make our way out of the hotel and head towards the mountain trail. My breathing already coming out chopped, I try to focus on the climb ahead, but unfortunately it isn't just the mountain that has my attention. Behind me I can hear Xander's own ragged breath. And maybe it's the strenuous exercise, but I swear that I can feel the heat of his tall figure.

At some point during the hike, he accidentally brushes against me and the contact sends a shiver down my spine, transporting my mind to places it shouldn't go. I try to fill the air with nonsense about how much I hate exercise so that this pent-up tension doesn't swallow me whole. My rambling is interrupted when I realise Xander has stopped walking and I turn around to look at him.

'What? You exhausted already? We've barely even started,' I wheeze. It has been more than two hours, so we must be close to the top.

'I'm fine. Just... can we keep moving?' He shakes his head, his eyes zeroing in on the ground, avoiding all eye contact. I squint my eyes suspiciously. The guy works out regularly, I doubt this is affecting him that much.

'I thought you were excited about this hike?' I question with a raised eyebrow. I give him a quick survey from head to toe, because this doesn't seem like the composed Xander

I usually know. It isn't until my eyes reach a *certain* part that I quickly avert my gaze and let out a weird squawking noise. Instinctively, I clasp my hands over my mouth. He doesn't say anything and instead just powers forward, pushing me along the path. The realisation that I can affect Xander *that way* fills me with a rush of giddiness and gives me the adrenaline I need to carry on.

I try to put him at ease with a new conversation. 'Be honest. With all the places you've travelled, this is probably the least exciting place you've ever been, huh?'

'Not really,' he mutters. 'It's beautiful actually.'

His eyes are intent on me. It's a good job I'm all sweaty and red from walking, otherwise he would see the blush that is fighting its way onto my face.

He looks hesitant before asking, 'Where's your favourite place?'

'You're going to laugh at me,' I say after a few beats.

'I promise I won't,' Xander says earnestly. He looks like he's being sincere, which throws me off. When he's thoughtful like this it makes it hard to remember why this guy has been my rival for the past few years.

I carefully consider my words. 'It's actually a place I haven't been yet…' I say shyly, looking up at the beautiful blue sky to avoid his gaze. 'I've always wanted to go to Japan – specifically to Kyoto. It's been on my bucket list for ages, but I've never had the chance. But maybe one day with the love of my life.'

'Why Japan?'

'I mean there's lots of things,' I say with a shrug. 'The culture, the history! I just know it'll be amazing.'

I think of how silly it sounds. For my favourite place to be an idea, somewhere I've imagined countless times but never been. Typical romantic dreaming. I remember how Theo used to make fun of stuff like this, saying I needed to stop imagining and start living in the real world. He did that a lot. Took the things I loved and wanted away from me bit by bit until I barely remembered myself. I don't want Xander to rain on my parade too, so I warn him, 'Don't crush my dream.'

As if he can read my thoughts, he replies, 'I won't. Promise.'

We keep hiking and are quiet walking alongside each other. A gentleness has evolved between us that feels new but precious. We are almost at the top when Xander breaks his silence. 'My favourite place was always my grandmother's house. I've been lucky to see a lot of the world, but it's the one place I've ever felt at home.'

'Your grandmother's house?' I can't keep the surprise out of my tone.

'Yeah,' he says softly. 'My parents... they never really wanted me around. I guess they didn't want kids to stop them having their own lives. I had my nan though, you know how I said we were close, well, when I wasn't at boarding school, I spent the rest of my time at her house,

111

which was practically most of my childhood…' He trails off, clearing his throat as if to try to escape from the memories of his past.

'Anyway, it's simple. She always made me feel like I mattered even when my parents didn't care. It was my sanctuary, really. But she's gone now and we sold the house, so…' He trails off wistfully.

The weight of his words hangs heavy between us, and I try to hide the sadness from showing on my face, but I must not have been quick enough.

'Don't,' he snaps, his voice sharper than I've ever heard it. 'Don't feel sorry for me, Yara, I'm still the same guy I was ten minutes ago.'

I nod slowly and turn my head so he can't see the pity in my gaze. Actually it wasn't so much pity, more sadness and anger. Sadness because I yearned to give that little boy a hug and tell him that sometimes we don't choose our family and that we can find our own family when we get older. And anger at his parents, because how dare they bring a child into the world and just discard him like he's nothing.

I don't say anything else after that and we continue our climb in silence, each of us lost to our own thoughts. By the time we reach the top, the tension between us has shifted. It isn't gone but it's changed, like a current beneath the surface of water. We finally get to the pub at the top of the mountain and I look down at the view, which is breathtaking, an incredible undulating landscape beneath

112

our feet. Mountains and valleys for miles around. Glittering pools and clouds that skim the highest peaks. But I'm too distracted to really enjoy it, my mind abuzz with everything I've learned about since this morning.

Chapter Thirteen

Three Weeks Left

The evening air is crisp as Xander and I stroll up to the entrance of the pub, the light flickering an amber glow above us.

My heart flutters when I feel Xander's hand fall on the small of my back, guiding me gently towards the door. His fingers flex as if he's holding himself back. But remembering how much walking behind me affected him earlier, I lean back into him, which elicits a low murmur from his throat. Yep, still got it. We're playing a dangerous game here and I think he knows it because his hand drops away quickly. The wooden door creaks as I swing it open, the warmth from inside welcoming us like a cosy hug. It smells faintly of the fresh-cut logs burning in the fireplace that sits in the corner. I can hear the faint hum of conversations from the back but, looking around, I see the pub is nearly empty. Another couple are sitting near the bar chatting quietly over their drinks. I stumble on that thought. *Another couple.* Obviously, I just meant *a* couple.

Before I can turn to Xander to see where he wants to sit, the bartender appears in front of us. The guy is pretty tall, almost as tall as Xander, with muscular arms covered in tattoos peeking out from under his sleeves. His face is handsome in a rough sort of way, but unfortunately I only have eyes for one person in this room right now. *The guy who almost sabotaged your career? You sure know how to pick 'em, Yara,* I mentally chastise myself.

But that doesn't mean I'm blind and I don't miss the way the bartender's eyes slide over me with interest, lingering a moment too long. 'Table for one?' he asks, flirtatiously. I feel the air shift as Xander stands taller and his body tenses. He lets out a barely audible scoff and I elbow him discreetly.

My eyes flick to Xander and then back to the bartender, my lips curling into a playful smile, trying to bring lightness to the situation. 'Table for two actually,' I say quickly.

The bartender blinks and looks a little surprised. A guilty smile spreads across his face. 'Ah, sorry about that! Didn't think you were with her.' He laughs awkwardly, barely making eye contact with Xander, who stands stoically. I elbow him again to try to get him to ease the macho energy. As the guy makes his way back behind the bar, he says, 'Go ahead and sit anywhere you want. If you're getting food, my mum will be over to take your order.'

Xander leads us to a small, intimate table near the back of the room. It's perfect. It's secluded enough for us to focus on each other, but still close enough to the other patrons that we have a bit of the pub's atmosphere.

I glance across the table at Xander, who is still seething about being ignored.

He must see the glimmer of humour in my eyes, which sets me off in a fit of laughter.

'I swear to God, you and your giggles,' he says in a low voice, his lips curving into a reluctant smile. 'That guy was practically drooling over you.'

'The poor bloke was just doing his job. Flirting is how you get tips. It pays the bills. Plus, he was super nice! He's given us the best seat in the house.'

'Right,' he says with a straight face, his voice dripping with sarcasm. 'A bartender who is just doing his job who doesn't even see me standing there. You could've said something, you know.'

Could've said what? I think. *Ah, sorry, Mr Bartender. This is Xander, my work rival, who, by the way, almost got me taken off the finale, but who somehow manages to send my pulse racing. In another universe, we'd be madly in love with each other, but in this universe he has a fear of love and connection because of childhood abandonment issues, so we'll never want the same things. Please, Mr Bartender, stop flirting with me. It upsets him, even though he doesn't want to be with me and never will.*

I chuckle to myself. Let's keep this light. 'Um, I did say something,' I reply. 'You heard me when I said "Table for two", didn't you?'

He pulls the menu from the table to hide his expression, but I can see his smiling eyes over the top. He must have realised how ridiculous he's being. After a few short moments perusing the menu, a woman approaches our table. She's an older lady who looks at us with a warm and friendly smile. 'What can I get for you two tonight?' she asks.

She pauses for a second, contemplating her next words, trying to figure out what Xander and I are to each other. Colleagues? Friends? A couple? *Her and me both*, I think. 'Are you two celebrating something special tonight?'

'Oh God, no!' I loudly exclaim, my hands fluttering all over the place in embarrassment. But at the same time Xander leans forward and says, 'Yes! We're actually celebrating our five-year anniversary.'

My eyes bulge at him. This charade again? First we were boyfriend–girlfriend in the hotel lobby and now we're five years married. He does like to move fast.

He turns things up a notch by reaching over and gently placing his large hands over mine, keeping them firmly in place. 'Ignore her,' he says, flashing the waitress a charming grin that does wonders. 'She likes to joke around like that sometimes. Me and the missus are celebrating five wonderful years together. We gotta keep the magic alive somehow, right?'

I kick him hard under the table, which doesn't deter him, in fact his smile widens as the waitress gives us a knowing look. Her eyes twinkle with a mixture of amusement and approval. 'Oh, how lovely! I knew you guys must've been together for a long time. It's the way you are around each other.'

We place our order and she says, 'I'll be back shortly with your food... and there might be something special on the house for you too, lovebirds.' She winks and walks away.

I let out a small sigh and glare at Xander from across the table. That whole interaction was so embarrassing for me, but he clearly doesn't feel the same because he is looking pleased as Punch with himself.

'Was that really necessary?' I ask, unimpressed.

'What, scared of a bit of fun? It's not like anyone's going to check – plus we're practically an old married couple anyway, aren't we? The way we bicker all the time. And maybe we'll get some free dessert for it, my long-suffering wife.' He stretches back in his chair. As he does, his top rides up slowly, revealing his very chiselled, tanned abs, but I quickly avert my eyes, hoping I haven't been caught.

'I can't stand you sometimes,' I say teasingly.

'Yeah, but you love me for it, Yazza.' He smirks.

I try to kick him under the table again but this time he sees it coming and dodges it at the last second.

The night passes quickly after that, with no awkwardness between us. As we eat our food, any discomfort fades as we joke around and share stories. The mood is light and for once it doesn't feel so... complicated. Xander was right about dessert, and we get a pair of chocolate melting-middle puddings courtesy of the kitchen. We have to suppress our shared giggles as the waitress pipes, in chocolate, on the plate in front of us: Congratulations! Here's to another five.

When we finish our meals, Xander tells me to head on out while he sorts the bill for tonight's dinner. I try to insist on paying but he is having none of that and shoos me outside, which has our waitress swooning for him even more.

It's peaceful at the top of the mountain. There's the coo of some birds wishing each other goodnight and maybe the rustle of some creature moving from here to there, but little else. I hear the crunch of gravel as Xander approaches from behind, and I turn to smile at him. We walk side by side in a comfortable silence, heading to the cable car that will take us down. After a while I spot something ahead. I squint my eyes and see that it's the cable car station. Xander breaks the silence.

'Ready to head back?' he asks in a small voice that breaks me out of my thoughts, testing the air between us.

I nod slowly, slightly shy because I realise we are about to spend the night together. 'Yeah, but I'm still laughing about your face earlier with that bartender,' I say with a snicker.

'You're a menace.' He grins at me.

I shrug smugly. 'I know.'

As we both get in the cable car and the doors close behind us, the world outside fades away.

Chapter Fourteen

Three Weeks Left

God, am I glad to be back at the hotel. I walked enough to last me the entire year! The minute I step through the doors to our room I feel a rush of relief. After a long day of trekking through muddy trails, the only thing on my mind is a nice, hot shower.

'I'll go first,' Xander says. Clearly as eager to get clean and wash the grime off as I am.

'No, don't worry. I'll go!'

'Oh, come on, Yazza, I called dibs first, plus I'm already halfway there,' he protests. The pleading in his tone doesn't make me feel a hint of sympathy.

'Dibs? What are we, five? Look I know we've both had the same trek but ladies first, right?' I raise my brow and cross my arms. I can't believe I just pulled the gender card, but I'm desperate.

He looks at me as if he can't believe those words are

coming out of my mouth. 'Yeah… but I'm a guy so I'll be faster.' Something in my stance must tell him that I'm not going to budge. 'Fine. You can go first. I'm only offering because, like the gentleman I am, I'll be gracious and wait.'

'I don't want to hear any complaining about how long I'm in there. It takes a lot of *maintenance* to look this good,' I say, gesturing over my muddy clothes.

Xander slumps onto the edge of the bed with a huff. 'I'll just be sat here… minding my own business.'

I gather everything I need and make my way towards the bathroom, but not before tossing him one last daring look over my shoulder. 'Yeah, you better!' I throw back at him. A teasing smile tugs at my mouth.

'Make sure you shut the door properly.' Xander raises an eyebrow, which sends an unexpected warmth through me. I hurriedly enter the bathroom and gently close the door.

I rush to turn the shower on until all I can hear is the soft hiss of water pelting the ground. While it warms up, I peel off my grimy clothes. Every inch of my body aches from the hike. I can't help the sigh of relief that escapes my lips as I step under the warm water, feeling it cascade over me.

I let myself relax as water clears away the mud and dirt from today. It feels good, incredible, actually. But something tugs at the back of my mind. Is Xander really going to just sit there and '*mind his own business*'?

My eyes drift towards the small crack between the frame and the door, which I may have accidently-on-purpose left slightly ajar. It's just a tiny gap that leaves enough room to see the vague outline of his figure on the bed. He's taken off his shoes and lain back. His feet sway from side to side.

It's as if he can feel me looking at him, because suddenly he sits up and moves towards the end of the bed.

I feel my heart skip a beat and I quickly snap my head away from the door. *Was he staring? Did he like what he saw?* Gah! No. I need to get my head out of the gutter. And I'm still mad at him. Sort of. We need to talk about it. I don't know what I'm feeling right now.

I quickly wrap up my shower, as not even the cold spray of the water can cool me down now.

I step out into the room, and halt at the sight before me. My mind can barely process what it's seeing. *Oh my God.* The man has been carved by the gods. I'm met with Xander's bare chest, with his jeans riding low on his hips, a towel slung carelessly round his neck. The sight has me drooling slightly but I try to snap out of it as a soft gasp escapes me. In pure embarrassment, my hands fly up to my face of their own accord.

He looks completely at ease, slightly amused by the inner turmoil that I'm currently experiencing. A grin curls at the corners of his mouth.

'What?' He cocks his head. 'You can't tell me you've never seen a shirtless guy before?'

I feel my face suddenly become hot and flushed. 'I uh... no. I mean yes, but—'

Xander is standing in front of me with utter confidence and my eyes can't help but track over every exquisitely carved detail of his body. I can feel my breath catch in my chest. Why does he do this to me? Is this just another way he's trying to get a rise out of me?

My mind is racing and I know I have to move. I can't just stand there like a puddle of mush in the middle of the room. No. I have to *do* something. 'I'm just gonna…' I grab my things and dart around him with haste.

Xander heads into the shower and the door slams shut behind him. I can still hear his damn chuckle. This man will drive me insane.

I take a steady breath and set my things down, trying to calm the whirlwind of thoughts spinning through my mind. The memory of him standing there shirtless, looking almost edible, doesn't help me feel any less dizzy.

My hands shake as I reach for my toiletry bag and start doing my skin prep. How the hell can I share a bed with him tonight after *that*? The thought of having to lie next to him after seeing him so… exposed… It makes my stomach flip. It's not as if I have never shared a room with a man before. But this? I'm sorry to say that, as cute and nerdy as Theo looked when we first got together, I never had this extreme physical reaction with him. Since I met him, Xander has been able to do things to my brain that I just can't explain, and now my body has apparently joined the Xander party. This is a completely different experience for me.

I rummage in my bag for my PJs. My only relief is that I know I packed my comfiest, and ugliest, set. Even if I'm drooling over Xander, I know he certainly won't feel the same way about me in these tatty, penguin-patterned pyjamas... Where are they? They're not here. My mind flashes back to when the girls came over and helped me pack – so quickly that I realise now that I can't be completely certain what went in.

I yank out something that looks familiar and, *oh*, I'm going to kill Maddie when I see her, because what I have in my hands aren't the granny pyjamas I thought I'd packed. No. These are my *nice* pyjamas, the silky form-fitting set that I usually reserve for *special* occasions, as in the set I only wear when trying to impress someone. Not that I've had much cause for that lately, with my exacting work schedule. A baby-pink pair of shorts and a matching cami with a lace trim that leaves little to the imagination. I scoff out loud and beg the universe to *kill me now*. Who brings sexy pyjamas to a work trip? With these on, Xander's going to think I was trying to impress *him*.

'Seriously?' I mutter to myself. 'Out of everything I own, she just had to go and pack these?'

I look again in my bag. No other options. I'll just have to sleep in these. The thought of wearing them in front of Xander makes my hands go sweaty. What he will think of me. How he'll look at me. And maybe, just maybe, a part of me does want to impress him. Or at least for him not to hate what he sees. 'No,' I say. I start to pace back and forth, shaking my head. 'Yara, *focus*, you cannot be thinking about that.'

I quickly change, and look in the mirror at my reflection for a few moments.

Another thought hits me and a strange impulse takes over, something I can't control. Hesitantly, I reach for my make-up bag on the counter. *Just a little lip gloss,* I reason to myself. I throw my hair up into a messy bun and take a last look at myself in the mirror. Not half bad, if I do say so myself.

My focus shifts to the bathroom door. The thought of Xander being in there, water running down his body, makes me feel some type of way. But I'll keep it to myself. He doesn't need to know.

'I can do this. Not a problem. None at all,' I whisper in denial.

Xander finally steps out of the bathroom but I daren't look at him because I don't trust my reaction seeing him in just a towel… or worse, in just boxers. An unwelcome thought enters my head. *How does he like to sleep?* Oh God, what if he sleeps naked. I'm panicking as I walk towards the beautifully made bed.

I'm lost in my train of thought when my foot catches on one of the pillows that has been thrown on the floor.

'Oh no!' I yelp. I stumble forward with my arms flailing all over the place to try to catch myself, but there's no point. I fall face-first straight onto the floor, and I lie there collecting myself. I groan, wondering what are the chances that maybe, hopefully, he didn't see that. I'm not left in suspense for long, because I hear his beautiful, booming laugh from behind me.

'Nice move! Really graceful.'

I start to pull myself upright, holding on to the edge of the bed. 'This is all your fault!' A flush creeps up my neck. 'Who the hell throws pillows in the middle of the floor like that anyway?'

'What? You can't just make accusations like that with no proof! I didn't throw them on the floor,' he says. 'They just... happened to end up there.'

My eyes narrow at him as he rushes over to help me. I try to right myself and he grabs my wrist but, in that split second, I lose my balance again. This time I manage to pull him down with me, and we both collapse onto the floor in a tangle of limbs.

My body collides with his and the impact sends a wave of heat through me. We're in a fit of giggles together on the floor. Xander is giggling! It's actually kind of a nice sound, the sort of noise I want to bottle up in a jar and save for later. He's normally so serious, reserved, but here we are being silly together. When our laughter dies down, all I can feel is the pressure of his chest against mine. In the dimly lit room, our faces are so close that I can see the glint of... *something* in his eyes.

'I, umm, I like your pyjamas.' His voice has gone kind of husky. When he speaks like that, it's too much to look at him, so I direct my eyes towards our feet.

In the tussle, I realise, my silk top has ridden up slightly, revealing a sliver of my bare stomach. Xander notices too. I see him hungrily run his eyes down my body. I can feel an electric tension between us. He goes to gently straighten my top, but pauses before he touches the fabric. He meets my eyes, silently asking permission, to which I nod. Gently, his hand pulls down the top, his fingers grazing my skin ever so slowly, making a jolt of energy go through me.

His mouth is parted slightly as he takes a sharp breath, trying to steady himself. His eyes have darkened and his pupils are dilated. It sends a shiver down my spine. He glances towards my lips. Head tilting to one side, I mirror him. There's an irresistible magnetic pull, drawing us ever closer. I flutter my eyes closed for what's going to happen next, preparing myself for the wave of feeling that I'm sure is about to break. I feel him move, his body shift closer, and then… nothing. My eyes fly open. Just as quickly as it happened… it's over. Xander pulls himself back, breaking the tension between us.

'Well. That was definitely… something.' He clears his throat, trying to dissipate the desire that's still thick in his voice.

What just happened?

We stare at each other for a few beats. I'm waiting, for

what I'm not sure. Finally, he speaks again. 'I'm sorry.' He closes his eyes. 'I… I didn't mean to—'

'It's fine,' I interrupt him. I don't want to know what he didn't mean to do. I don't want him to tell me that it was all a mistake for the second time.

Before he can say anything else, I jump to my feet and into bed. I grab my Kindle and quickly settle under the covers, needing a distraction. I hear Xander moving around the room, going back into the bathroom, locking it. He's brushing his teeth. I think of his rounded shoulder, his strong bicep, the light brown hairs tracing down to his wrist, his large hand holding the brush, manoeuvring it back and forth. I stare at the same page of my latest Mafia romance, unable to take anything in. Ten minutes later I feel the dip of the bed as he slides in beside me…

'Goodnight,' I say softly. I click to the next page on my Kindle, despite having not read a word. I just need to do something normal, everyday, to get me through this weird weekend.

The subtle stirring of birds outside only heightens the quiet in the room. His voice is mellow and low as he says, 'You know… If you're feeling awkward about – about sleeping close to me, we can always—'

'*Don't*,' I stop his sentence. 'Don't worry, okay? We're fine. *It's fine.*'

Xander lets out a loud sigh and turns away from me. I worry I've done something wrong. Why did he put the brakes on so suddenly? He turns out his bedside lamp. I'm so conscious of all his movements, the bed wobbling as he adjusts to find a comfortable position to sleep in.

'I just wanted to say... I had a great time today,' he says quietly. 'I know you might not feel the same way, but I really like being around you. I like being your friend.'

My heart skips. He has no idea how happy that sentence makes me. I've only ever wanted to be Xander's friend, to have a writing buddy, someone to bounce ideas off. I hate having a work rival, the competition I feel like he forces us into. I try to stay cool, calm and collected. I keep my voice steady. 'It was fun.'

It was more than fun, I know. Being with him in this way, flicking between the ridiculous to the flirtatious, from joking to vulnerable and back again, it feels electric.

I finally put my Kindle away, having made no progress on my book, and turn out my lamp. We lie there in the darkness, our unsaid words hanging between us. I know he's awake and he knows I am too. It's an awareness of the other's energy, as though our thoughts are fizzing from his mind to mine. The room is awake, alive with it. I roll onto my side, and I feel him turn over and pull my body close to his, holding me. In his arms, I can feel his warmth. Who knew Xander, cold as ice in the office, could burn with so much gentleness? In the safety of his embrace, my eyelids begin to droop, the heft of sleep falling heavily on top of me. As I drift off, I hear him whisper, 'I wish things could be different.'

Chapter Fifteen

Three Weeks Left

My eyes flutter open to the warm sunlight that has filtered through the curtains. I stretch out my arms and a small groan escapes my lips. Yesterday's events come flooding back to me and the exhaustion from the hike is still throbbing in my bones. That was probably one of the best sleeps I've had in a seriously long time.

Waking up in an unfamiliar bed, I blink a few times to get my bearings. Something feels *off*. My gaze darts around the room. It's too still. There's no soft breathing next to me, no scuffing of feet across the thick-carpeted floors. The bed is empty. I'm alone. Where the hell is he?

I shoot up from the bed and take a good long look around the room. Has he really done a runner? When nothing even happened? Just a weird almost-kiss. A sharp feeling of panic grips me in a way I didn't expect. It's strange, really. How Xander's unexplained absence makes me feel more vulnerable than I care to admit.

So many different thoughts run through my mind. I try to push the negative ones away. He probably just went out for a walk... Although I, for one, have had more than enough walking. He wouldn't just leave without telling me... *would he?*

But then all my worst fears hit me with full force. What if he is just... *done*, with me, with us? Is there even an *us*? Does he regret what happened last night? Holding me in my sleep? Telling me he liked my pyjamas? I look down at them now. My stupid pink pyjamas. Was it all a mistake to him? Am I just another awkward situation to run away from? Like he does with everything, with everyone else?

My mind spirals out of control. Each thought bulldozes the next in a frenzy I can't stop. I furiously rub my face. There has to be an explanation. My hands slam down on the mattress and suddenly my fingers brush against something.

A crumpled piece of paper.

With a frown I hold it up and carefully unfold it. I let out a sigh of relief as I read the words scrawled across the page:

Gone to get brekkie, back soon :)
Xander x

All that panicking was for nothing. *Oh, thank God.* It's fine, he's just gone to get breakfast. My stomach unclenches and I allow myself to close my eyes and sink back into the bed.

I reread the note. *For someone so smart he sure does have the handwriting of a little boy.* A small smile tugs at my lips.

The events of last night play like a movie in my head. We'd got so close. My heart flutters and my body gives an involuntary shudder remembering how it felt when his gaze deepened as his eyes traced the contours of my hips, my waist. How my breath caught when our limbs had become tangled with one another's. His soft murmuring voice in the dark. When he said how much fun he'd had, how much he likes spending time with me.

The question though is, *Where do we go from here?* I don't know how we're meant to act together now. Was this just a one-time thing or would it happen again? Would we ever be this way again or when we get back to the office will it be business as usual? Is he agonising over this situation the same way or is he indifferent to the whole thing? Having spent a day with him out of the city, out of work, I know that he's nowhere near as blasé about things as he pretends to be.

I clamber over the super-king-size bed and grab my phone from the bedside table. Maybe a dose of the real world will give me some perspective. I run through the list of people I could talk to about this. I can't call my family, not even Elif. They would want to know everything and there is really nothing to tell. *Kinda.* A few looks, some jokes exchanged, a night spent side by side. I mean, what would I even say? *Hey Mum, hey Dad, I'm currently being tortured by inappropriate thoughts of my co-worker who has this weird aversion to love and will probably never see me as anything other than a friend – and if we're really getting down to it I think friends might be an overstatement. Oh, and also he tried to sabotage my career, which you both hate. Mustn't forget about that little tidbit.* Yeah. Absolutely not.

I decide to talk to my friends instead. I tap on Amira's name and hit call and then invite Maddie as well. As the phone rings, I bite my lip nervously.

'Hi, Yara, everything okay?' Amira's voice comes through first. Judging by the grogginess in her tone, it sounds like I've just woken her up. Her face pops up a millisecond later and my suspicions are confirmed when I see the bleary look in her eyes. A twinge of guilt hits me in the stomach. Maybe I should've just waited. Maddie joins the call.

'Hey, girly, what's up?' she says, unusually high-spirited for this time of day.

'Were... were you with someone?' I can't help the curiosity nagging at my brain. It's the only thing that makes sense.

'Wha—I... No! Why would you even think that!' She lets out a forced laugh that increases my suspicions further. It's clear she doesn't want to talk about it, so I drop the subject for now.

'Right… Basically I just woke up. Xander's gone to get breakfast and I don't have long to chat before he gets back,' I say.

Maddie laughs while Amira covers her mouth in shock. 'No way,' they both say simultaneously.

'What?' I ask, surprised. What are they both *no way*-ing at?

'I take it you two finally caved, huh?' Maddie says with a smirk.

Her words hit me and I stare at her in shock. *Finally?* What does she mean by that? The question suddenly makes everything feel a bit more… complicated. I mean more than it already does. Why would she think we'd slept together?

'Oh God, no. No! Nothing like that,' I rush out. Although I guess it was a little something like that – wasn't it?

It's as if I hadn't said anything because Maddie carries on, 'Well, it's about damn time. You've both been dancing around each other for *way* too long.'

My mind races at this revelation. 'Maddie, what are you talking about? What do you mean *dancing around each other*? I mean sure! We had a nice time yesterday. But I can assure you *nothing* happened. At least, not in the way you're thinking—'

'Uh-huh.' This time Amira cuts me off. 'So, you're telling me nothing happened? C'mon, Yara, don't bait us. You are *wayyyy* too worked up for "*nothing*" to have happened. We can see it in your face.'

'Well, we…' I worry I can't describe it. It's not about what happened but how it *felt*. The static that buzzes between two people who can't stay away from each other. 'We didn't do anything. Me and Xander, we… just spent some time together and it was surprisingly nice. That's all.'

I'm not ready to tell them about the almost-kiss. It's too humiliating to put it into words. How it felt explosive and like everything I ever wanted and, then, he just… stopped. Got up like nothing happened. Leaving me on the the floor.

'Right… okay,' Maddie says slowly. 'So, are you telling us you didn't feel anything at all? No connection? No tension? There's always been something between you two disguised beneath this supposed *rivalry* of yours.'

I contemplate her words. Something inside me has cracked open and it's like I can't stop the flood of emotions that have broken free. What if Maddie and Amira are right? Am I just pretending like it didn't matter?

'Well, we had the long drive and we were just so open with each other. Then, we went on a hike and had dinner together and it almost felt like a date, but it wasn't. And to be honest I haven't felt this…' I pause, thinking about my next words carefully, '…at ease with someone in a *really* long time but the thing is I'm scared, you guys. I can't—'

I feel my throat catch. Emotion rises in my chest. What if Xander ends up being another big disappointment?

'Oh babe.' Amira's voice drifts softly over the phone. 'We've been waiting for you to finally admit it to yourself.

Truthfully, me and Maddie, even Andrew, thought you two had some sort of thing brewing between you. So, if it makes you feel any better, we've all noticed.'

Feel any better? I think it makes me feel worse actually. How can everyone in my life see something between us, but Xander can't?

'I—no…' I stutter. I shake my head frantically. 'I just don't know if I can take that step with him, you know… He's got things of his own he needs to face and what if he never does? What if it's just a phase to him? What if I'm just not enough? And I can't forget about what he said to Meagan. That worries me.'

'If this is about Theo, you've gotta move on from him eventually, Yara,' Maddie says firmly. 'I'm not saying you should jump into something straight away with Xander. But if that is what's holding you back and you're afraid to get close to him because of what happened, you need to know that not every guy is the same. Sometimes you have to take a leap of faith.'

I feel a slight tightness in my chest at the mention of Theo's name. I put a hand to my face. The last thing I want to do right now is talk or even think about my ex. I'd been avoiding the topic for so long, but my friends have helped me realise that I'm not entirely over him. Or I am over him, but maybe I've not completely healed from his betrayal.

'I haven't thought about Theo in ages,' I say. And it's true. I try to remember the last time I really thought about him, the last time I stalked his or his girlfriend's social media pages. If I had to say, it would probably be around the time me and Xander started working together. My eyes widen at the realisation.

Amira has just started to say something when a shadow passes in my peripheral vision. Is it an intruder? I freeze and my blood runs cold for a split second before my eyes settle on the dreaded 'intruder' and my body relaxes. There in all his glory is Xander, holding a paper bag in his hand.

He doesn't say a word, just watches me with a calm, knowing expression. His gaze flicks between me and my phone in my hand.

A wave of anxiety crashes into me and my face flushes with embarrassment. *Oh God, how much has he overheard? What if he heard everything?*

I rapidly comb through everything I can remember saying in the last couple of minutes. 'I'm so sorry, girls. I need to go. Let's catch up soon,' I say, my voice tight as I end the call.

After a few moments he breaks the silence. 'I-I um… brought you your favourite, almond croissants,' he says. 'I hope you're hungry.'

He dangles the bag in front of me.

'You seem to know a lot of my favourite things.'

Xander hesitates before he drops his eyes to the ground, suddenly shy. 'We've known each other for a long time.' His voice is quiet. 'You learn a thing or two about a person.'

'Knowing someone a long time doesn't mean you remember all their favourite things. Like what's Meagan's favourite pastry? Or Andrew's? You've worked with them for longer than me.'

He smiles. 'I notice what's important.'

I look up at him, surprised that he would admit something that makes him seem so sweet and vulnerable. There's so much kindness in his expression, a quiet but urgent request for my approval. I'm not sure how to respond, but I find myself giving him a genuine smile. I can't decipher all the feelings currently flowing through me. Desire. Confusion. Frustration. I'm supposed to stay mad at him, after what he did, but right now I can't find it in me. We can deal with all that messiness once we get back to the office.

'Eat your pastries and get ready, we should probably get on the road soon. I saw a nice café on the way back here. We can get some writing done before we head back,' he says all of a sudden. 'Three weeks of solid work and we can get a draft to Meagan.'

Ah, there he is, that's the Xander I know, who loves to avoid any subject that involves real emotions. I can visibly see the walls start to build back up slightly, like he's already bracing himself for the worst-case scenario. That hurts me more than I care to admit but I'll be okay. I always am. With that he leaves and the room gets noticeably colder. Perhaps it's a sign of what's to come. Maybe I shouldn't let myself get too used to him.

Chapter Sixteen

Three Weeks Left

Xander drives until we reach a cute café nestled in the woods, seemingly in the middle of nowhere. It reminds me of a fairytale cottage, hidden away from the world. Xander suggested this place as somewhere to get some work done before we head back home... back to reality.

The Kabin. *Huh, original.* I snort with a chuckle and Xander's lips tug up slightly and he touches my shoulder as he opens the door for me. Inside, the café is an oasis of cosiness. Wood-panelled walls, a crackling fireplace, a mismatch of soft sofas and armchairs in different colours, with cushions and throws strewn across them. There are huge bookcases lining the walls, full of dusty-looking hardbacks and well-thumbed holiday reads that backpackers have discarded. Peaceful. It's the perfect escape from the whirlwind of emotions I've experienced since Xander picked me up yesterday morning. I close my eyes and breathe it in, and all I can think is, *Wow, this is a writer's paradise.*

I spot a nice area by the window with two chairs and a large wooden table and make my way towards it. I make a comfy makeshift office for us, getting out my laptop and ordering a large black coffee for him and a chai latte for me.

I take a quick look at Xander, who has taken the seat across from me, pulling out his signature notebook. A pile of loose papers spill onto the table, and I watch closely as he arranges them into some sort of order that can only make sense to him. His brow furrows in concentration and his lips purse slightly. It's a cute, boyish expression that makes my heart glow. I've always admired that Xander can absorb himself in his work, eventually emerging with an incredible solution to a plot problem all the other writers have been pondering for days.

The longer I watch him, the more I feel a creeping sense of dread. The trip is coming to an end. We're going to drive back tonight. Will he look at me, talk to me the same way when we get back to London? I know so much more about him now, why he is the way he is, and I've seen his vulnerabilities. And he knows about me and my ambitions and how much I want to make my parents proud in a career they don't understand. We can't just forget those things about each other, can we?

141

This feels like a precious moment, and I want more of them. There's so much unresolved between us. Yes, we still have the finale to finish, but there's everything else too. I'm still trying to figure out my feelings, but now one emotion stands out above all the rest, one that I'm unfortunately familiar with. Fear. I'm not sure how to deal with Xander and the way he can just retreat into himself at times, shutting me out without communication. Or the way that every time we seem to make progress, becoming friends like he said, he still keeps me at arm's length.

Xander looks away from his notes and catches my eye. 'You got anything?'

I clear my throat and sit up straighter in my chair. 'I do. I've been thinking about that scene we couldn't agree on, the ending between Layla and Atticus. I think maybe we could...' My words trail off and I pause as I navigate putting my idea into words.

'Yeah?' Xander looks at me intently. His attention is completely zeroed in on me, which makes me squirm.

'What if Atticus betrays Layla, like you said. But instead of it being an all-out betrayal, we later find out that it's for her own good?' I get to the edge of my seat, starting to talk more passionately because I really think *this is it*. 'Like... he has her closest advisor, Elaria, assassinated. Layla is devastated to lose her companion, but little does she know that Atticus actually does it because he believes it's the only way to keep her safe. Because Elaria was a traitor all along and was planning to get Layla killed, but Layla will never find that out.

'Layla wants to believe that he would never do that to her, never stoop that low, hurt her that much, but couldn't he? He is the villain after all, so she has her doubts. He wants to reveal everything to her, but he can't… at least not yet, which would be a great plotline for the next season. That way we still have the betrayal plot but it's still giving the fans a sprinkle of the love story they want to see! It's romantic and tragic at the same time.'

Xander is silent as he processes my words. I scan his face for some sort of reaction. His expression doesn't give much away. But then his eyes light up, and a spark of excitement makes those stupid butterflies in my stomach erupt.

'Wow, that's… a great idea,' he says with something akin to admiration. The look in his eyes takes my breath away, because over the years he's never looked at me like he is now. Like he's truly *seeing* me.

'The complexity of it really gives the characters depth, which will leave the audience wanting more. Will he ever find a way to reveal the truth to Layla before it's too late?' He scrabbles through his papers as he starts threading the plotlines together. 'It's morally dark. It raises the question – who has the right to rule? When viewers see how it all plays out, they'll realise how Layla's reaction in the next season shapes her future. As well as what it means for the kingdom.'

'You really think it'll go down well?'

'I know so,' Xander says with such assertiveness that it fills me with complete confidence. 'It's definitely a bit of a shift from what we originally had planned... But that doesn't mean it's a bad thing. You should write it, though. It's your idea. It'll be amazing.'

'You sure you're okay with that? With me taking the lead on this scene?' I ask, the memory of that meeting with Meagan hitting me with full force.

Xander casually leans back in his chair. 'I don't mind. You came up with the idea, it's only fair that you get to run with it.' He shrugs as if it's as simple as that. Maybe it is. 'I know I've gone on about top billing, but may the best writer win, right?'

My mind is already running through all the possibilities of how I should write the scene. It feels good to be on the same page as him.

He's scribbling furiously at his notebook as I start typing up the last scene on my laptop. He looks up to ponder something, his beautiful face turning towards the fireplace. The flames cast undulating shadows over each of his features, highlighting them anew for me. His sharp nose, his curious green eyes, his strong brow. A question creeps into my mind and I feel we're in a good enough place for me to ask, 'So... How did you get into writing?'

His hand pauses mid-air over his notebook. I want to know more about him. I want to know everything I can.

He takes a moment before he responds. 'I guess… I have this need to understand,' he murmurs. 'I've always had an interest in stories but, when I started writing, it was because I wanted to make sense of… certain things. Things I couldn't quite figure out on my own because I didn't really have anyone to ask. All sorts, emotions, relationships…' He looks at me, before saying carefully, 'Love.' He pauses. 'I mean that one obviously hasn't been my forte.' He lets out a sarcastic laugh before his gaze rests on me again. 'But I think… I think I might have a better understanding of it now.'

If someone had told me two months ago that we'd be sitting across a table from each other, not only getting along but talking seriously about love, I wouldn't have believed them. In fact, I would have probably laughed in their face. But here we are.

We stare at each other for a while, neither of us wanting to break the spell. I hadn't expected so much honesty from him. I wish we could just stay here in this intimate café. I could almost believe it's our living room. The piles of books. The warm glow of the fire. Him, me, sharing a table to write on. This could be us, for ever.

After a few solid hours of writing, we've drafted about half of the finale. With the outline that we developed back in London, I'm confident we'll be able to deliver a full draft before the deadline. There's a sleepy atmosphere in the café and we still have to drive back to London, so we make a plan about who's going to take the lead on the remaining scenes. We agree, though, that we'll collaborate throughout the process. Meagan was right. This trip really has got us into the flow of working together.

Feeling satisfied with everything we've accomplished on the trip, I lean back in my armchair. As casually as I can, I ask what's been playing on my mind since our hike. 'You ever think you'll change your mind about love? That two people – two characters, I mean – could maybe find each other and stay together?' I can't decide whether I want him to hear the hope in my question or not.

His eyes are serious as he peers at me. 'I don't know... Maybe?' He sounds uncertain. 'Writing with you, it's taught me new ways of seeing the world. New possibilities. But I'm still not sure if I'm ready to believe in it right now. At least not in the way other people do. I don't know if I ever will.'

I can see the silent apology in his gaze. I look down, not wanting him to see the heartbreak I feel cracking across my face.

I tighten my fingers round my pen. The clasp cuts into my palm and I welcome the bite of pain – anything to distract me from what I'm feeling right now. 'I get it. I do,' I reply softly. It isn't a lie either. I've been burned before, but the difference between me and him is that I'm willing to move on and I don't know if he ever will.

So, that's that, I guess. He's not sure. At least I know. I don't want to break this tentative alliance that we've built over the past two days, but there's no point now in putting it off any longer. The question I should have asked him the second I got back from Meagan's office. I have to know.

'Xander... can I ask you something?'

His eyes flicker to my face. He smiles, fondly but sadly. 'Sure. Anything.'

I finally let out the words I have been keeping caged all weekend. 'Why did you go to Meagan and claim my idea as yours? I've been racking my brain to understand, but I don't get it. We were fine at Andrew's party, but then only a few days later I come into work only to find out you went to our manager behind my back. I don't understand, please help me understand.'

At least it's all out in the open now.

Xander's jaw tightens and his expression hardens. I feel a prickle of sweat at the back of my neck. Despite the fire, a cold chill sweeps over our table. I hold my breath, waiting for him to respond.

'What are you talking about?'

'Meagan told me that you had come up with a great *romantic* resolution to Layla and Atticus's plot. You know that was my idea. You stole it.'

'I *stole* it? You really think I would do that to you?' His voice rises but I can see him trying to remain calm. I catch his trembling hand but he clenches it into a fist. 'Is that what you think of me? I know we have this stupid rivalry game we play at work, but I thought it was just a bit of fun. I'd never steal another writer's idea, and definitely not yours. Especially after—' He lets out a laugh of disbelief and rubs his hands down his face.

'What else am I supposed to believe? We were the only people in the office that night, how else could she possibly have known? Why aren't you telling me the truth? If you just explain, I'm sure we can—'

'I'm telling you I don't know. But it doesn't look like you would believe me anyway. You clearly think I'm a liar and a cheat.'

'Don't put words in my mouth. I don't think that! But I know you'll do everything it takes to get ahead. You're ambitious. It's something I really admire about you, but I think you just went a bit far this time.'

'Fine. Yes. Yara, I went to Meagan behind your back and schemed this whole thing all so I could take the credit from you. I'm just as bad as you think I am... There! Happy? Isn't that what you want to hear?' His breathing is laboured and I can see the hurt in his eyes.

'I'm not asking you to tell me what you think I want to hear... I just want to understand,' I scream, on the verge of tears now. The chatter in the café has stilled. I catch a glimpse of the waitress behind the counter staring at us, frozen.

Something unreadable flashes in his eyes. 'I'm done talking about this. I think we've made enough progress for today.' He shoots up from his chair and starts collecting his notes. 'I think it's best we work separately from now on.

You write your scenes and I'll write mine, then we'll just try to tie them together after. I wouldn't want to be accused of stealing more of your ideas.' He won't look me in the eyes.

In a flurry of paper, he edges past me, and heads out the door towards the car.

What the hell just happened? He seemed to have no idea what I was talking about. But why then did Meagan tell me I need to up my game? Why did she think the romance plot was Xander's idea? Does it even matter now? I want to take back the question because I'm pretty sure I just ruined everything. Xander hates me and there's no way we'll be able to Frankenstein a great finale from a bunch of disjointed scenes.

I've already done enough damage and I don't want to keep him waiting any longer, so I fold up my laptop and follow him out of the door.

Neither of us says a word on the long drive back to London. It's unbearably tense. Over four hours of radio silence. I keep glancing at him from the corner of my eye, hoping he will give me something. *Anything*. But he just stares ahead, as though I'm not there at all.

I turn my head towards the window to hide my face and press my forehead against the cool glass. My mind replays everything that happened this weekend, all our time spent together. It was going so well until it crashed and burned.

As we get closer to home, the ache in my chest expands until I worry it might suffocate me. Whatever we had built on this trip has been broken. I don't know if I can fix it. Or even if I should.

A single tear rolls down my cheek and I feel more lost than I've ever felt before.

Chapter Seventeen

Two Weeks Left

Ever since the Snowdonia trip, the days have been a complete blur. Mine and Xander's relationship has been put in a tailspin. In the past few weeks, we've gone from rivals to friends to something more, and finally emerged as something even worse than before. And I can't get him to talk to me.

No matter how hard I tried not to, I've found my thoughts drifting to him. I try to keep myself busy, burying myself in my scenes, but everything just feels... *wrong*. It's not just that he won't talk to me; it's like he's going out of his way to avoid me. This morning he's working from home, which he does as much as he can now. When he has come into the office, he hasn't so much as spared me a look, which is honestly impressive when our desks are right across from one another. I would give anything to go back to the way we were. I miss the banter, his stupid smirk that wasn't exactly a smile, the teasing glint in his eye when he was up to something. The list goes on.

What I hadn't expected is just how *alone* I feel without him. I hadn't realised how comfortable we were as colleagues. How much I looked forward to seeing him every day, even when we butted heads. There are so many things that we still have left to say to each other. We never spoke about that almost-kiss in the hotel room, and now we probably never will. It will be another open wound between us that just festers. I need him, I realise now. We work well together. I'm going through the worst writer's block of my life and the best writing partner I've ever had is suddenly cold and distant with me. It's breaking my heart. Breaking my heart in a professional sense, of course. Oh, who am I kidding? We're well past professional at this stage. It's breaking my heart in every way.

I thought I had experienced heartbreak before... but it was nothing like this.

My desk starts to vibrate as my phone buzzes, which pulls me away from my dark thoughts. I grab it, thinking it could be Xander, but when I glance down at the screen I see that it's my mum. I try not to let the disappointment sound in my voice when I pick up. I step away into the dimly lit corridor.

'Yazza, honey, it's been a while. How is everything? We miss you!' The sound of Mum's voice greets me like a warm hug.

'I miss you too...' I reply as I try to keep my tears at bay. God, I hadn't realised just how much I needed some comfort, a reminder of home.

We catch up on everything... Well, not absolutely everything. I can't tell her about Xander. Especially now. Too many almosts and what-ifs. Not worth mentioning.

When it gets towards the end of the call, the conversation drifts to where it always goes. 'Are you still working on that writing stuff of yours?' Dad's voice joins the conversation. 'Or have you started looking at getting a real job?'

The familiar sting of their disapproval pierces me deeply, no matter how hard I try to stop it. It's the constant reminder that even though I'm working my dream job, which I'm damn good at, it will never be enough for them. They'll never understand why I've pursued a creative career path when they always pushed me towards a 'proper job'.

'My job is going fine, Dad, thanks for asking,' I say. 'I've actually been given this huge opportunity to write the season finale with a – with a colleague. Our names will be at the start of the episode. It's going really well so far.'

My heart aches as I speak about Xander and our project, but I swallow the hurt down.

My mother sighs as she prepares to give the same speech she gives at the end of every call. 'That's lovely, Yazza. But you know how volatile this career is. Opportunities come and go in a flash. We just want you to be in a stable and safe job. Something with a real future. You're not getting any younger, you know. Did you get my email about law school?'

With everything else going on, this certainly isn't helping. I can feel the burn of tears at the back of my eyes. I refuse to let them see just how much it pains me. I love my parents, I really do, but this topic will always be a sore spot.

'I'm happy with what I do… okay? Just stop.' My voice breaks slightly.

There's a pause on the other end, then my dad speaks up. 'You're not going to listen to us… are you?' His disappointment is palpable over the line.

I can't bear to carry on this conversation any longer. 'Speak soon, love you.' My voice feels raw as I hang up.

I bury my face in my hands to try to calm myself. My chest feels like it's getting tighter and tighter with each passing moment. My parents' words echo through my mind, the reminder that I'll always be a failure in their eyes. The wayward child that they can't explain to their friends. Who works late for so little reward. No wonder Xander can't bear to talk to me. I disappointed him too, by taking Meagan's word over his. All I know is that something isn't adding up.

Taking a deep breath, I let the tears I've been holding fall. I'm lost in my own thoughts when I see some movement in the corridor from the corner of my eye. Oh God. *No!* Anyone but him. I must have done something horrendous in a past life because this has to be some kind of karmic joke.

Xander.

His eyes lock on mine from across the corridor. I can see him holding himself high, aloof, above it all. But there is a flicker of worry for just a second.

I quickly turn my face away. I don't want him to see me like this, in my moment of weakness, not now. Not after everything that has happened between us recently. What if he thinks I'm crying about him? I almost want to call out, *oh this, don't worry, this is nothing to do with you! Just crying because I'll never be enough for my parents and I can't shake the crushing weight of their disapproval. Nothing to see here!* I make quick work of wiping my tears as fast as I can.

His voice echoes along the corridor. 'Yara?' His tone is cautious.

I quickly whirl round. 'I'm fine. Please leave me alone.'

I spin on my heel and head towards the door, desperate for any sort of escape.

The second I put my hand on the door, Xander reaches out and grabs my arm. With a firm grip he pulls me back into him, the world coming to a stop as we are finally face to face.

I peer into his eyes and there is no trace of anger. I search his expression for any judgement because that's the last thing I can handle right now, but I only find a kind, searching look in his face. Wordlessly he pulls me into a hug. Not the sort of hug you'd offer a stranger in need, but a heartfelt gesture, full of care and concern. It's exactly what I need and I…

I. Just. Break.

The floodgate of tears I have been holding back for *so long* pours out of me in waves. I can't pinpoint one reason I'm crying. It's my parents, my job, the pressure, the finale, this city, Xander. The cumulation of all the events that have led to this moment hit me all at once.

I breathe in his scent. Xander doesn't say anything. He doesn't need to; him being here when I need him is enough.

I'm unsure how much time has passed when the tears start to subside and I feel normal again. Well, as *normal* as I can with everything going on.

I peel myself out of his arms and my eyes dart around, looking anywhere but him. I can't bear to see how he must be looking at me. I probably look a pretty pitiful sight.

'Um, thanks,' I mutter. The air around us stiffens, goes stale. I can already feel his walls going back up.

'Well…' He clears his throat. 'See you around.'

And, with that, he walks away.

The tension between us snaps back with brutal force, hitting me with a brutal dose of reality. We are not friends. He doesn't trust me any more. Every step he takes away from me is like a whip crack to my heart.

Chapter Eighteen

Two Weeks Left

I stand there for a while and stare at the spot where Xander has just been. After I manage to pull myself together, I head back to my desk.

It's hard to ignore the whispering from people as they glance between me and Xander. It seems like we've been the talk of the town lately. Everyone heard about our trip and now they all see that we're not talking. It's just like the day when Meagan pulled me into her office and everyone seemed to know I was in trouble before I did. I've had enough of this. I never wanted to the source of the office gossip. I just want things to go back to how they were.

I glance over to Xander's desk but, to my surprise, he looks just as adrift as I feel. My mind flashes back to the moment when we had that argument in the café, and all I can see is that hurt expression on his face. I hated seeing him like that. I knew how much it took from him to open up to me. And for some reason my accusation was a betrayal to him.

I'm so lost in thought that I barely notice Meagan come up to my desk.

'Hiya, Yara!' she says. 'How's the episode coming along? Two weeks to go! I'm looking forward to reading.'

'Yeah, it's... getting there.' The words sound hollow even to me.

'If you need anything. Anything at all, you know where to find me. I'm always here to help, even if you just need someone to talk to, okay?' She sounds concerned. Clearly Xander and I haven't been pretending to work together as well as I hoped.

I nod absently. But then my thoughts start to spiral. How are we supposed to finish the episode when the guy can barely look at me? My eyes drift towards today's date on my computer and I groan at the reminder of how quickly the deadline is approaching. We got a lot done before Wales but, now we're writing separately, I have no idea whether it will all come together. For all I know, Xander could have changed his mind about what I suggested for the final scene and be writing his own new version... what if we can't agree on the final draft when there's no time to spare?

As I watch Meagan's retreating figure, I know that I have to figure out a way to get Xander alone, somewhere he can't avoid me. There's too much at stake – my career, the show, whatever friendship we ever had – for me to just let this go.

The moment I see Xander get up from his desk, I seize my opportunity to follow him. I track his movement until he disappears round a corner. I get up. But I take a different route that will lead me to the vending machine, where I know he'll be. He always goes there around this time of day for a snack, probably a Twirl, and this may be my only chance.

I intercept him just before he reaches the vending machine and latch on to his arm, then drag him with me into the small storage cupboard at the end of the hallway.

He looks surprised but quickly recovers. 'Is this really necessary?'

I close the door of the small room. It's dark and cramped, with only a single hanging lightbulb above us. All around are stacked papers, tipped cartons that spew pens over the shelves, and a random sword that someone from props must have left here. 'Yes. Yes it is. We *really* need to talk. Sorry about this' – I gesture to the messy storage cupboard around us – 'but I feel like everyone is talking about the finale and how we're doing and there's so much *pressure*.'

I look down and see my other hand is still gripping his arm. I hadn't realised just how small this room really is, hardly any space between us. In the stress of the moment, all I could think about was finding somewhere to talk. But now that we're here, a wave of nervousness hits me in my stomach. We're close. I can feel the heat emanating from his chest. The buckle of his belt strays dangerously close to my waist. I look between us again. Yeah… definitely too close.

He looks down at me expectantly. 'Fine, you wanted to talk. So, talk.' There's an undeniable hostility in his tone, which drives the knife deeper still.

'We're running out of time. You know it, I know it. The deadline is coming up hard and fast and, if we don't finish it, we're both screwed!' My words are frantic as I try to get him to understand the urgency of the situation. I finally gather up the courage to look up at him, my eyes scanning his, trying to gauge his reaction.

But what I find in his gaze devastates me. He's looking somewhere past, through me. 'We?' He lets out a cruel laugh. 'There is no *we*, Yara! You…' His breathing is laboured now. He runs a hand through his black hair. Scrunches his eyes closed. 'You made sure of that.'

I feel nauseous. Dangerous to be nauseous in such a small cupboard where my mouth is almost touching his shoulder. I want to escape, get out of here, go somewhere far away. But I can't. This means too much.

Instinctively, I place my hands on his chest. 'Can we just—Can we just stop for a moment. Please, Xander?'

When he doesn't reply, I barge onwards, 'It's not even about who is going to get the stupid lead credit at this point. But if we don't hand in a draft of the episode then our jobs could be at stake. This isn't about *us*.' I pause to consider whether I want to say my next words. I bite the bullet. 'Even if you want to continue pretending that there isn't an *us*.' There, I said it. But I'm too scared of his response, so I quickly move on, 'Whatever I said that offended you, we need to get over it because we were always meant to do this together. We make each other better, I *need* your help... I-I *need* you.'

'I'm sorry, Yara. I don't think we can make this work. I read the scenes you emailed over, they're good. I'll write mine and we'll fit them together. I just think we're better off on our own.

'And there isn't an us. Seriously. It's like I said in Wales. I don't believe in love. You do. You'd be better off with someone who can give you what you need. I don't know, maybe I thought that was changing.' He looks into the distance, laughing breathlessly, 'But I was right not to. Giving yourself over in that way, it leaves you open to hurt. Because look at all the hurt we've caused each other. You can't force me to change my mind.'

His words pierce me. Every type of relationship we could have had, whether as colleagues, or friends, or whatever else I might have wished for, has been ruined. Clearly our time in Wales affected him as much as – if not more than – it did me.

'I know,' I say, my voice barely audible. 'And for the record, I didn't want to force you to change. I-I like you just the way you are... most of the time anyway. I like you when we're arguing about whether *Barbie* or *Oppenheimer* was the better movie. I like you when you're scribbling ideas in your *terrible* handwriting in your notebook. I like you when you eat your afternoon Twirl and you spill flakes all over your desk.' I let out a sad laugh. I glance up at him and he's softened, looking bashful after my compliments. 'I just – I really didn't want us to end like this.'

'Like what?' He edges ever closer to me in the small space. His words curl around and into my ear. 'What is it that you want from me, Yara?'

The tension between us shimmers. The air shifts. I look up at him and my lips part. I see his gaze dart to my mouth. His eyes darken, just like they did in the hotel room just before he...

'I—' But before I can get the words out, Xander's lips clash onto mine and I let out a yelp of surprise that dissolves into a sigh of relief. His tongue brushes against mine. He clasps his hands round my waist, as I hold him by his hips, colliding in a flurry of passion.

There is nothing gentle about it. It's like all the energy of the hours, days, *years* working across from each other suddenly explodes, at last a release from all that pent-up longing. It's desperate and urgent, our problems forgotten for as long as we're together like this. For now, we are just two people, lost but connected. His fingers tense, tightening the hold on my waist, pulling me impossibly closer.

I can't focus on anything but him, on how much I want this – how long I've *wanted* this. How long have

I secretly desired him? I can't even think. The room spins and nothing else matters. Slowly, his hand trails upwards and finds its way to my throat. His fingers gently press into my skin. Not hard enough to hurt but enough that the sensation makes me gasp. I move my hands up to his head and entwine my fingers in his hair. He groans slightly as I tighten my grip, pulling him deeper into the embrace.

The shrill blare of a ringtone snaps us both back to reality. Xander yanks himself back as if my mere touch would suddenly scorch him. He runs his large hand through his hair, which is now dishevelled, falling messily over his green eyes. God, he looks incredible.

He looks at me, eyes still heavy with lust. The small cupboard is filled only by the sound of our ragged breathing. He bites the inside of his cheek and then clenches his jaw. 'Uh, I-I shouldn't have done that.'

'What?' My voice breaks and I hate myself for it.

Instead of replying, he steps back from me, backing himself into the corner of the cupboard as far away from me as possible. 'We can't... *I* can't do this, Yara.'

My head reels. 'What are you saying?' I can't stop the tremble in my voice. 'You can't keep doing this to me. *You* leaned in for a kiss. *You* pulled me in and now you're just going to pretend like that didn't happ—'

'Just forget about it... I already have.' He casts his eyes at the ground, looking ashamed. 'You wanted to come in here to talk about the episode. We've done most of it anyway, it's just that last scene, so let's just propose our own endings and see who comes out on top.'

'You're a coward, you know that,' I spit out. 'I get that I might have upset you before, but you *do not* get to use me as an emotional punching bag, just because you are too scared to face your own feelings.'

He stumbles back as if I've just hit him. His face is full of regret and hurt. Before I can say anything else, Xander is gone. The door is burst open and our dark cupboard is suddenly full of the bright fluorescent lights from outside, the cacophony of sounds of everyone bustling around the office. Photocopiers humming, bubbling chatter, a coffee cup clinking as it's placed in the sink. But for me, it's deathly silent. Because he's not here.

My mouth still throbs from our kiss, the best kiss I've ever had. I can't go out there, not yet. My legs give out as I sink to the floor. I don't know what I expected bringing him in here. But that was certainly wasn't it. My heart is breaking all over again but this time I'm also angry. *Screw him*. If he wants to lash out like a child, then fine. But I will have no part in it.

Chapter Nineteen

Five Days Left

For days afterwards, I try to forget the storage room incident and get on with my version of the final scene. But I keep being hit with waves of the memory of that kiss. God! That kiss. I groan into my hands. How his green eyes lit up when he looked at my lips and everything that came afterwards felt inevitable, just as it should. The way his hand pressed the nape of my neck, the soft skin that prickled under his touch. How good it felt to have my fingers tangled in that hair. But that memory doesn't exist without everything that came afterwards. I can't forget how Xander shook me off and left me alone, once again.

Despite how much he's hurt me and how much I've hurt him, I do what I always do when things get tough. I block out the world and throw myself into work.

If Xander and I just can't write together, he's right that this is the only way to move forward. Two endings. Meagan chooses the best. But I can't imagine Meagan liking the idea when we present it to her. It's against her ethos. She always says the best writer doesn't exist, there's only the best *writers*. It's a team effort that makes great TV, with a sprinkle of competition. I agreed with her, until now.

Today is Monday. We have a meeting this afternoon where we'll present Meagan with our endings. Maybe the fact that we're presenting it today, rather than leaving it till the end of the week, will encourage her to give us some grace? I'm not hopeful.

I have a rough version of the scene I pitched to Xander in the café and I'm racking my brains on how to make it better. Not just better, something I can be proud of. This is far from it. It just lacks *something*. That energy that makes characters come to life. The thing that Meagan has always said I'm good at, I guess. But I feel like since the storage room incident last week, I've been forcing myself to write in frantic bursts, as much as I can until another Xander memory interrupts my progress and forces me back to square one. It's so frustrating. I bet he isn't agonising over me the same way I am him.

I stare at my screen, the curser taunting me as it blinks on the half-full page. For a moment all I can hear is Xander's cruel words. *Just forget about it… I already have.* My only solace is that he didn't mean it. He's always pushed people away. He told me that: how difficult he finds it to be close to his parents and sister. He can't trust anyone. How arrogant of me to hope that I could break the cycle. I look up to the ceiling, taking a minute to steady myself. *Enough, Yara*, I tell myself. I am stronger than this and I won't cry over any man. My phone buzzes, which snaps me out of my thoughts. I look down to see it's a message in the girls' group chat.

Amira: hey u okay? you haven't replied to any of my or Maddie's texts. we r worried about u. pls talk to us. did something happen with Xander?

I contemplate her message. Yes, I called Xander a coward, but I've been one too. My friends have sent me a flurry of messages over the last few days and I've sent them half-assed replies, just enough to let them know everything is fine and I haven't been murdered. I've been so preoccupied with Xander that I've become a terrible friend. I know I need to explain what happened but I'm not ready for that just yet. My thumb hovers over the screen as I think about how to respond.

Me: All good. Just the final stretch before we meet with Meagan later today... speak soon xoxo

My phone buzzes again.

Amira: ok we'll stop badgering you... for now haha. good luck 2day!! x

Before I can type out a quick thanks, Maddie sends a message in that chat.

Maddie: me and Amira were thinking drinks later? you in?

Another message comes through.

Amira: you're not allowed to say no btw :D

I smile at their messages, grateful for the offer. Maybe I should go, even if it's just to forget about work for a few hours...

Me: Count me in! Wish me luck girlies x

I look at the clock and realise it's almost time to meet Meagan. Whatever I have here, I guess it's going to have to do. I rush to get my copy printed.

The thought of sitting side by side with Xander, Meagan across from us as she reads, *compares* our work, makes my stomach feel knotted and tight. Too late to do anything about it now. I can only walk to her office with my head held high. Soon, all this will be over, and I can move on to something new at last.

I find Xander waiting outside. His piercing gaze locks with mine for just a second. We both hover by the closed door of Meagan's office, looking at the ground, anywhere but at each other. You could cut the tension with a knife. And still, my heart flutters, nervous around him. I want to kick myself for being hopeful that he would just do something... anything to make this better.

Xander reaches for the door but his hand lingers on the handle. He cocks his head at me and I take a good long look at him. He looks really worse for wear, the worst I've ever seen him actually. Still unfairly handsome, but there's a hollowness to him. His hair is messy. The bags under his eyes really stand out. He looks like he hasn't slept in days. His clothes are less attractively dishevelled than normal and more just, well, normal dishevelled. When he's usually so well put together, it's strange to see him in a crinkled, shrunken shirt that doesn't fit right with trousers that don't match.

I blink a few times. Maybe I was wrong and he has been struggling as much as me. He parts his lips as if he is about to say something. My blood hums in anticipation. Is he going to apologise? Profess his feelings to me as if we're in some sort of rom-com? That would be a stretch, but a girl can dream.

The beginning of a sentence escapes his throat, but he stops himself when Meagan swings open the door.

'Yara! Xander! How are you both feeling? Come in, come in.' Meagan ushers us inside. Her cheeriness jars with whatever exists between me and Xander. She picks up on the dissonance and her eyes flicker nervously between us.

She takes her seat and her smile immediately fades as we place two separate scripts on her desk. We both retreat into the cavernous armchairs opposite Meagan's large desk.

'What's this?' She lets out a confused laugh.

I squirm as she disdainfully fingers the two scripts, as though we've just dumped our leftovers from the canteen on her lap. Xander speaks for us, 'We encountered some creative differences when approaching the ending and I thought it'd be easier this way. The scripts are eighty per cent the same. We made good headway in Wales, but we wrote the rest of it separately. I told Yara that you should pick whichever one you liked best.'

I turn to him. I press my lips together to hold back my surprise. He's taking full responsibility. I thought he'd taken the credit for my idea but now he's taking the fall – maybe I was too quick to judge Xander's actions?

Meagan's brow rises. She sighs. 'I have to say that this is disappointing. That's not what I expected from either of you. I wanted you to work *together* on this, because I think of my writers as a *team*. Do you know how much we have riding on this? This is the finale of our most-watched show – twenty million viewers and counting – and you're acting like children. This isn't some sort of game. I put my neck on the line to give you this opportunity.' She shakes her head at us.

'Do I have to remind you of the *junior* part of your job titles? I could have given this to your more experienced colleagues, but I thought you were ready. I knew how much you wanted this. I see the two of you at your desks, bouncing ideas off each other. Xander, I've seen how much Yara has helped you improve your characterisation, and Yara, your plotting has come on in strides since working with Xander. All that analysis the two of you do about *The Wire* and *Bridgerton* and whatever else, it's made you so much better over the years.

'I thought you could play to each others' strengths, but instead you've succumbed to your weaknesses.'

Meagan's words are heavy and I can feel the weight of them pressing down on me. She presses her beautifully manicured fingers into her temples, massaging them fiercely.

Xander begins to speak, but she puts her hand up to cut him off. 'Sorry, Xander. I'm in no mood for excuses,' she says tiredly. She pushes the two scripts to the edge of her desk. 'Let me save us all some time. I'm not going to read either of these. I know they won't be your best work.

'You have until the end of Friday to figure something out. Let me make it very clear this time round, seeing as there was some *confusion* before. You either submit something *together* or don't bother handing anything in. And if that doesn't work, it might be tight, but I have a roster of talented, senior writers who will be able to pull something together. And that'll be the last time I take a chance on either of you.'

Her ultimatum hangs in the air. The pressure of it threatens to suffocate me. I close my eyes and take a couple of deep breaths, swallowing back my guilty tears.

'Glad to know that we're all on the same page. I expect to hear from you both soon.' With that, she stands, leaning over her desk and indicating that the meeting is over.

Xander gets up first and exits the room with his head hung low. I start to follow him, but Meagan's voice stops me in my tracks. 'Yara, can I have a quick word?'

I freeze. Xander turns back and gives me a fleeting but reassuring look before she shuts the door behind him.

'You and Xander...' she says. 'Something's going on, right?' Meagan's stern tone is gone, and now it's gentle, coaxing.

I look sharply at her in surprise and want to bury my head in the sand. *This cannot be happening.*

'I've watched you work together for three years. I'd have to be blind not to notice' she says, her voice filled with knowing.

I fight to keep some sort of composure. 'There's nothing going on... not any more anyway.'

'Who are you kidding? I see the way he looks at you... and you, him.' She nods her head from side to side. 'Look, this show is about a lot of things. But the thing that makes you so good on the team is you've always understood that, most of all, it's about love. The kind of love that makes you feel alive. It's rare. The kind of love that's worth going to war for, literally in the case of *Claim to Power.*

'You and Xander are both great writers, but brilliant TV needs a human heart. I know it was unorthodox, and I'm now wondering whether it was a mistake, but I have to admit that there's another reason why I put you and Xander together for this finale. This is a show about love and – call me old-fashioned – I've always believed in that old adage that the best writers *write what they know.*'

She puts a hand on my shoulder and lowers her head to look at me seriously. 'Do you understand what I mean?'

I'm struck by everything she has revealed to me. The significance of it all. I feel the walls closing in around me. I say the first thing that comes to mind, because it's what caused this mess in the first place. 'I know Xander came to you to try and take the credit for my idea. The romance plot.'

'Yara, what...' Meagan looks as confused as I feel.

My eyes prickle with tears. I will not, cannot cry here. I've already lost enough of her respect by handing in a shoddy script that she was wise enough not to read. I can't stay in this office a moment longer. 'I'm sorry, I have to go. Xander and I will have a new script on your desk on Friday.'

Before Meagan can respond, I rush out of her office and head back to mine and Xander's station. I need answers. No more whispers and assumptions. I need to know the truth. But when I arrive, he's already gone.

Chapter Twenty

Five Days Left

> **Me:** Sorry!! Meeting went... not great! Will have to pass on drinks ☹

I send the text in the chat and pocket my phone, ignoring the flurry of dings it makes in response. A bad friend. A bad writer. A bad whatever-I-am to Xander.

After work, I head to Lunar Books in need of comfort and a chai latte. I spot that my favourite seat by the window is free. No matter how many times I come here, that table always seems to be free for me, the refuge that's there for me when I need it. My fingers fiddle with the sticky laminated menu to distract myself. Xander and I have the rest of the week to pull our thoughts together. I think about what Meagan said after he left. She can see there's something between us. No matter how much Xander blows hot and cold, however much he tries to deny it, there is a connection that neither of us can ignore. We must have been more obvious than I thought. No wonder the whole office is talking about us.

I go to file Xander away in that corner of my brain I try to ignore: *Failed relationships*. With Theo, it had just been an endless loop of constant disappointment and broken promises. Afterwards, I'd spent *months* thinking to myself, why hadn't I seen the signs, when they were just so *obvious*? Even thinking of it now, I can feel the sting of the betrayal. And I was just beginning to trust Xander when his actions proved that, just like Theo, I can't and I shouldn't. I groan and wonder if maybe Xander's right. Getting close to someone new just opens you up to fresh but familiar wounds.

I thank the waitress as she writes down my order. I'm lost in thought, looking out of the window, when I hear the horrible sound of a chair screeching as it's pulled out, breaking me out of my trance. I realise it's coming from my table. I almost drop my mug in shock when I see who it is.

'Andrew?' My voice is laced with surprise.

He throws a smile at me, but it's oddly strained, not his usual cheery self. His cheeks are red and he's slightly out of breath, as if he's just run here. There's a deep crinkle in his brow and he can't stop his leg from fidgeting under the table.

'Is everything okay?'

'I was in the area and I know you mentioned this place before so thought I'd stop by.' His fingers twitch nervously. I decide to wait it out. If a weekend with Xander has taught me anything it's that, if you give a man some silence, eventually they'll tell you at least some of their feelings. Finally, he takes a deep breath. 'There's something I think you should know.'

'Okay…?' I say slowly.

He hesitates briefly before leaning closer. 'What's happening with you and Xander… I think—No, I *know* what went wrong.' He winces, as though bracing himself for impact. A hint of shame tightens his expression.

My stomach drops, a sense of dread rising. 'I don't… what are you on about?'

'I didn't think it was a big deal, and I wasn't going to say anything…' My hand grips on my mug like it's a lifeline. 'But I-I feel like you need to know. Meagan grabbed me as I was leaving the office just now and asked me to clear something up. It wasn't Xander who told Meagan about the initial details of the episode and your romance plot… It was me.'

What. I slam my mug down with an audible thud. It was *Andrew?* Now I know, I almost want to laugh about how little it matters. When I'd thought it came from Xander, it had hurt so much more to think of him trying to sabotage me. Because I cared for him. More than just cared for him, actually. But from Andrew, I realise I barely care – not about the job, the embarrassment, none of it.

As I struggle to figure out what this means, Andrew continues, 'At the party, Xander was explaining to me the disagreement you had over how the story should go. That you wanted romance. He wanted drama. Then, that Monday, Meagan asked me how I thought the two of you were getting on. I said that it was going well, and I had just been talking about it with Xander. Because I didn't want to reveal the argument to her when you were just getting started, I said that Xander had just been telling me about potentially resolving the story with romance. But now I realise how it must have sounded to Meagan, that it was all Xander's idea, and I'm so, so sorry that you didn't get the credit. I hadn't thought about it until Meagan asked me as I was leaving the office to explain exactly what Xander said.'

'Oh God.' I rub a hand down my face. 'It wasn't Xander.'

All of the pieces start to fall into place. Meagan's confusion when I said Xander had come to her. The hurt on Xander's face when I accused him. The memory sends a stabbing, guilty feeling through me.

'No... it wasn't. And it wasn't like I'd gone out of my way to say something... Meagan and I were just having a casual conversation and it just slipped out.' He flinches at the confession.

A chasm of regret opens in my chest, gnawing at me. No wonder Xander was so angry with me. He'd opened up to me in ways I suspect he hasn't with anyone else in a long time and I had assumed the worst about him. How will I make it up to him?

'I'm really sorry, Yara. I would've said something sooner but I hadn't realised things had got blown so out of proportion.'

'It's okay. Thank you for telling me. Everything makes a lot more sense now.'

I feel like an idiot. How many times have I yelled at the main character in my books to just *talk* to their love interest. But that's the thing about real life, not everything can go as smoothly. Why was I so quick to jump the gun? Why didn't I ask more questions? This could've easily been avoided if I had looked at the person in front of me, instead of letting my past hurts dictate my actions.

Yes, I was angry, but not at Andrew... no. I was angry at myself for always assuming the worst.

'Guess I can't blame him for avoiding me like the plague then.' I let out a humourless laugh, trying to keep my tears at bay.

'I probably shouldn't be saying this because he'd kill me if he found out. But... he's struggling just much as you are. I think he's had to face things that he's been scared to deal with his whole life and he's using this argument as an excuse to push you away.' His expression is kind, encouraging. 'But I know one thing: for the past three years, you're the only person he's ever wanted to talk about.'

I laugh. Him and me both, apparently. How many times have Amira and Maddie teased me for just how often I moan about 'my colleague who I just *hate*'. A million emotions swirl through me and I don't know what to do with this information. *Is it too late to fix this*? Do I even want to? I have feelings for a guy who doesn't believe in love. A guy who says that it's unrealistic and naive. If I try to patch things up, would he just push me further away?

'I don't know what to do, Andrew.'

'It wouldn't hurt to talk to him. Even if it is only to get some closure,' Andrew says.

Suddenly, I know exactly how to resolve all of this. I stand abruptly. 'I need to go.'

'Good luck.' Andrew's eyes glint with knowing.

The cold air hits me the second I step outside, but it's a welcome relief, focusing me on the present. I have to find Xander and talk to him. I'm not going to let anyone – Theo, Meagan, Andrew – decide what happens next. For the first time in weeks, I feel like I'm taking back control of my life.

Chapter Twenty-One

Five Days Left

I head back to the office, hoping that Xander will have returned to work on the finale. He prefers it when it's quiet and dark and he can concentrate without the disturbance of all our colleagues. We're alike that way. It's a ten-minute walk from Lunar Books but I get there in four. My heart is racing when I arrive at our desks.

But the office is empty. Xander is nowhere to be seen. *Where the hell is he?* I internally scream in frustration. I plop down on his chair, the whiff of his cologne making me dizzy. I'll need to corner him tomorrow morning, but will that be enough time? We already only have five days – basically four now as it's late – to present our joint effort to Meagan. I need him to talk to me.

But then, my eyes snag on a small note thrown on his desk. The writing, scribbled hastily, is unmistakably his.

Heart of Seoul. My favourite restaurant. Who is E? Is he seriously on a date? Wait, no. I've got to stop jumping to conclusions. *Look where that's got you so far, Yara.*

I check the time. It's 7.45 p.m. now. I could still catch him if I'm fast enough.

I could get the tube or a taxi. A taxi will be expensive, but hey, what's the cost of true love? Feeling like a British Carrie Bradshaw, I rush out of the office and flag down the first black cab I see. The whole journey, my eyes flicker anxiously to the time on my phone. I hope I get there in time. Otherwise, I'll have wasted an entire journey and a good chunk of money.

What am I even going to say? I want to shout at him. To yell at him for being so cruel. To confess how special our weekend in Wales was. To thank him for opening up to me. To apologise for misunderstanding the situation so badly. To pull him close and never let go.

I get there at ten past eight, not late enough that Xander will have finished his meal and left. I hope not anyway. Heart of Seoul is alive with activity. Table after table is filled with patrons, slurping noodles and struggling with chopsticks. There are smart waiters bustling between tables. The walls are dark wood, with low amber lights overhead. I realise, with a too-late sense of dread, that it really is the perfect location for a date.

I hurry into the restaurant, my eyes quickly scanning the room for any sight of him. For a minute I think he must have gone, but then I see him.

Xander... and there, right before my eyes, is what I suspected.

My heart sputters to a stop as I watch him deep in conversation with a girl about my age, huddled closely together. She's beautiful, of course. Long dark hair that she's tied into an elegant bun. She wears a sleek purple silk top that brings out her green eyes. There are diamonds in her ears that sparkle as she shakes her head, smiling, brushing her hand across his. An easy, familiar touch. I see him laugh, which causes an ache in my chest. In my experience, those deep, full laughs are rare. For him to be sharing them so easily with another woman, so soon after what happened between us, hurts more than I want to admit.

I remember now the skipping out of the office and how he almost missed Andrew's party because he was meeting someone. I can't believe how foolish I've been. This is the Xander I always knew, the womaniser. Sure, we might have fun for a few weeks, but this is what he does with everyone. I tell myself I need to look away, but it's like a horror movie. I can't.

Lost in an emotional fog, I realise someone has been saying 'Miss' repeatedly, and I feel a tap on my shoulder.

'Sorry, miss, are you waiting to be seated?' a waitress asks.

'I-uh, sorry.' I stumble over my words. 'I'm not staying actually... I'm just gonna go...'

The waitress looks increasingly blurry as my eyes fill with tears. Then, Xander looks up. He sees me and his face is stricken with feeling. I run out of the restaurant, my heart shattering more with every step I take. I don't even make it halfway down the street before I feel a large hand pulling me back. It steadies me as I gather my bearings.

Oh, please not now.

I don't even need to look up to know who it is because I would recognise *his* hands anywhere.

Xander.

Thankfully, my mind freezes before I let my emotions get the best of me. 'Get off of me!' I snap, which garners a few curious stares from onlookers.

I wave my hands in the air in an act of frustration. 'Look, I understand. It was silly of me to assume that we—Never mind. I know you're mad, but after everything we've been through I guess I thought... But it's probably too late now—'

'Now wait a second, Yara, just calm down. You—' he starts to say.

'Please, don't worry about it. I don't want to embarrass myself any more than I already have. I'll see you at work tomorrow. I hope you have a lovely evening.' I go to turn away from him, but again he drags me towards him.

'Yara, stop! It's not what you think, okay?' he says urgently. 'That's my sister.'

I blink frantically. I wish the ground would open me up and swallow me whole. 'Your... your sister?' I'm so mortified I wish the rain would dissolve me and I could seep into the drains. I think of who I saw in the restaurant and I experience a flash of recognition. Eloise. That same sister who followed me on Instagram all those months ago.

'Yes, Yara, my sister,' he says. 'We reconnected after my grandma's funeral. We've been having a few lunches and dinners here and there.'

My mouth opens but my mind isn't able to generate any words. Overwhelming relief floods me. And then, that same uncertainty, nervousness that I felt on the way here.

We stand facing each other on the street, cars racing past us. The streetlights illuminate his handsome features. 'So, did you come here for a reason or was it just to gape at me like a dying fish?' he teases, like we are back to how we used to be.

My mouth snaps shut at his observation. I take a deep breath, knowing that I just need to rip the Band-aid off and say it.

'About what I accused you of before I... Andrew explained everything and it's all a huge misunderstanding. I know you didn't try to take credit for my idea. But Meagan told me you did. Well, kinda. I mean at the very least it was heavily implied. I didn't know what to think and I'm sorry! Can we just be okay now?' I plead.

'I see.' He looks towards his feet, scuffing the ground with his heel back and forth. 'I told you that I would never do something like that. I hoped that you would believe me.'

'I know.' I hang my head and try to swallow the lump in my throat. 'I'm sorry. But, I guess I've found it hard to trust people. In the past. But it will be different in the future, I promise.'

'I feel like my word is never going to be enough for you.' His gaze rips away from me like he can't bear to look at me any longer. 'But why should it be? We've been rivals for years. If Meagan had implied you'd done the same, I probably would have believed her too. Maybe we've just been through too much together to properly let our guard down, y'know?'

He's talking himself out of us. I feel him slipping away.

'I think I was right,' he says, still looking at his shoes. 'The kind of love we imagined back in Wales, it doesn't exist. It wasn't real. How can two people trust each other that much? We clearly can't.'

'Xander, no, I—'

'It's okay. Look, I need to get back to Eloise. I have to think about... about everything. I'll see you at work. We have a lot to do.' He smiles weakly. He holds himself rigidly, not letting himself get too close to me. 'Get home safe.'

And with that he leaves me standing in the middle of the pavement staring after him like a love-sick puppy.

As I watch Xander's retreating figure, his words echo through my mind, the heaviness of the conversation settling in my stomach like a deadweight.

It doesn't exist. It wasn't real. But it does. It *was*. Because I felt it. We felt it. I'm certain of that.

Chapter Twenty-Two

One Day Left

All of Tuesday, Xander didn't come into the office. Meagan kept walking by our desks, glancing suspiciously at me sitting there alone. Yesterday and today, Thursday, were the same. I'm not really sure what I can do. We're supposed to hand something in tomorrow morning. With Meagan's ultimatum hanging over my head like this cloud of doom, I am stressed to the max. I've bombarded Xander with *very* professional emails, but he hasn't responded. Maybe he's just given up on me.

I am in my flat trying to tune out the relentless ticking of the clock hanging on the wall. Every tick that reverberates is a reminder of how quickly time is slipping away. I pull a blanket tightly around my shoulders and sink into the couch as I glare at my computer screen. I'm looking at everything we did up until the moment we fell out in the café. I've read the half-finished episode a hundred times and what's so frustrating is Meagan was right. Our writing styles had worked perfectly together. It had everything: drama, emotional stakes; it promised to give the fans what they wanted but would still surprise them and leave them hungry for the next season. I can't help the feeling that this could have been – would have been – one of the best episodes of television of all time, certainly one of the best in our show's history.

But it's over now. It will probably remain unfinished business – just like me and Xander. I've accepted the worst. Meagan is probably in her office right now drafting an email to the other writers she had in mind. I sink my head onto one end of my couch and let out a sigh. I say an internal goodbye to the thought of my name appearing at the start of the episode, to my parents saying congratulations, to all the opportunities that this could have opened up for me afterwards. To think I actually believed we could work together. My God, I'm such a fool.

But that's until...

A ping comes through my laptop. I brace myself for a message from Meagan telling us that *while she appreciated our efforts, as she has no confidence that we're actually working together and time is running out before we have to start production, she has made the executive decision to...*

I will myself to look at the screen, but what I see instead has me sitting up so fast I almost get whiplash. I have to rub my eyes to make sure it's real.

For a second, I just stare at the name, scared that if I blink it's going to change into something else. I blink. Nope. It's still there.

From: Xander Woods

I pause, my thoughts going a million miles an hour. My first instinct is to rush and open it, but my fingers hover over the mouse pad. *C'mon Yara*, I tell myself. I do want to know what's in that email, I really do. But I'm also scared. What if Xander says that we can't work together? He could be handing in his resignation tomorrow for all I know. Maybe he thinks it will be too awkward after my failed romantic gesture yesterday. I feel a pang of dread as I realise just how much I would miss him, not getting to see him every day. I force my fingers to move. I click onto the email.

The email is short, of course it is. Xander has always believed in that old bit of writing advice, 'Show, don't tell.'

Finale. It will only be better with you. ☺

It's small and ridiculous, but the smiley face warms my heart. It's so unlike Xander, or so unlike the Xander I knew a few weeks ago: serious, self-conscious, avoidant. A silly, sweet smiley face makes me realise how much my understanding of him has changed, how much our relationship has changed.

I bite the bullet and open the file, trying to ignore the pounding in my heart.

And then I begin to read...

I scan through most of the episode, already familiar with it as it's what we had come up with... together. Xander hasn't changed anything that we agreed upon up until our fall-out in the café. Then there are the scenes we shot back and forth over email. He's done a great job linking them, although they're not as good as what we wrote with each other.

My gaze halts at the start of the last scene. This is it.

Our two main characters, Layla and Atticus, are standing on opposite sides of the room. The meeting must take place in secret in the dead of night. As far as Layla knows, Atticus has betrayed her by having Elaria, her closest advisor and best friend, killed. She's heartbroken in more ways than one. She's grieving not just the loss of her friend, but the possibility of ever rekindling her relationship with her childhood sweetheart. But in reality he has only damaged his own cause, because Elaria was a double agent working for him. He has scuppered his own chances in the war to save Layla, his love's, life. The tension, anger and regret in the scene are palpable. The air is thick with words unspoken between the two of them.

The last thing Xander and I discussed about the finale was that Layla would never discover the noble intentions for Atticus' betrayal. A climactic, tragic end to the season that put their future romance, which the fans so loved the idea of, in jeopardy.

The conversation starts off slow, their words clipped. I'm struck again by just how good a writer Xander is, and how *great* a writer he has become in the past few weeks. Even without actors and costumes and elaborate sets, I can feel the emotional power of the scene. I carry on reading. Something in the conversation breaks. They start to open up to each other, to exchange barbed words. Gone are their aristocratic niceties and subservience to convention – these are two people in beautiful, complicated love, with jaded pasts, who've hurt each other in so many ways.

Tears gather in my eyes and the words begin to blur.

This scene feels different from the rest. I realise I know these characters, intimately, deeply. This isn't just Layla and Atticus... it's *us*.

It's all there. Everything that has led up to this moment, every sharp exchange, every hesitation, every moment of vulnerability between them... between *us*.

The ache in my chest deepens as I continue to read the last few lines of this scene.

33.   CASTLE SET INT. PRIVY COUNCIL CHAMBERS
      DAY 30. 20:35

Atticus:

I have to confess something. Elaria. I know you're hurting. But she was not your friend. She wanted to have you killed. She had to be eliminated.

Layla places a hand to her chest, forced backwards with the weight of this reveal. She recovers herself, stands taller, trying to force some authority into her voice.

So, Xander changed it. He thought Layla should know what Atticus did for her. Interesting. My eyes scan the page furiously, desperate to discover the rest of the story.

Layla:

But why? If she was an ally to your cause, why would you do that? Why would you get rid of her?

Atticus laughs, a dark, hollow laugh. There are tears in his eyes. He spins on his heel.

Atticus:

After all this time, you really think I don't care about you?

Layla:

You're the one who walked away! You pushed me away, you did this!

Atticus:

Because I was scared!

I am so invested. I can practically hear Xander saying those words. Hear the raw and frustrated emotions as they pour out of him.

What happens next makes my heart flutter. After a few beats of silence, the two protagonists reach for each other...

And they kiss. Their first kiss since their youthful romance, when they were running around the palace gardens. I can see it perfectly. A kiss of reunion. A lost love finally brought together again.

I put my hand over my mouth to stifle my gasp. I'm not surprised by this in the context of the story. This is what I had wanted for them from the start. No. I just can't quite believe that it was Xander who wrote it. A scene filled not with swords and politics, but emotion. Passion. Romance.

I finish reading and think, *Wow, the ending is the best part.* It's like Xander has woven every single unspoken feeling between us into this scene, a confession that whatever we had was real and shared. I scroll down to the end of the document. And there, in the margins, Xander has left a comment: 'Sorry for changing it slightly from what you described. I thought that Layla should know how Atticus feels.'

Xander's final scene fills me with so much hope. Maybe we can actually get this done by tomorrow morning. And perhaps we can even make something work between us.

I can't waste another second and so I jump up from the sofa and run to my wardrobe, almost falling face-first tripping on days' worth of discarded clothes. I yank open the wardrobe and quickly grab the first outfit I can find. I throw on a baby-pink jumper with a pair of blue jeans. Looking in the mirror, I give myself a nod of approval, proud of what I've managed to put together under such stress.

I can hear my own heartbeat as I make my way to the door. I will my hand to stop trembling as I reach for the handle. I will go to him and we'll finish this episode together. I have doubts, of course. Will he really be ready for me? Will he be ready to open himself to love; not only that, to potential hurt too? But the moment I open the door, all my feelings of uncertainty vanish. Because there he is, standing on my front doorstep, the man who has been occupying my thoughts for so long, in all his six-foot-three glory.

He looks gorgeous, one hand leant against the doorway. He's out of breath, as if he ran here. He wears a pair of worn dark blue jeans and a Strokes T-shirt.

But when I take a closer look at his face, I see the haunted look in his eyes. His hair falls over his brow, but it can't hide his concerned expression. He straightens slightly and, when his gaze finally meets mine, I'm hit with an invisible force of feeling that's so strong I have to take a step back. I almost laugh. I'm just like Layla.

'Oh my God, Xander? What are you doing here? Have you been waiting out here in the cold?' I shout at him.

He laughs, the sound like music to my ears. God, I missed that sound... I missed him. The smile fades as he looks at me more intently. I have the prickling sense that whatever he's about to say might change everything.

'And I would've waited for you, however long it took,' he says, with a gallant look. Despite myself, I feel a flutter in my chest at his Prince Charming declaration. Then, he snorts. 'No, don't worry. I'm not a stalker. I just got here.'

I nervously chuckle, wiping my hands down the front of my jeans as they start to sweat profusely. Remembering he's standing out in the cold, I move back, motioning for him to come inside.

'Did you get my email?'

'I did, yeah.'

'And did you see the ending.'

'Yes.'

'The whole thing?'

'Of course.'

He nods, looks down, suddenly shy. 'Sorry, I just couldn't wait to hear what you thought. About everything.'

Xander walks past me and heads into the room, his eyes drinking up the details of the space eagerly. He takes in my patchwork blanket, my toppling bookshelf that I've been promising to organise since I moved in, my *Hereke* rug that my *anneanne* gave to me when I visited her in Turkey last summer, the prints that Maddie and Amira bought me for my birthday. It hits me properly then that Xander is here. In my home. In my personal space. It takes everything in me not freak out. I'm struck by just how much he looks like he belongs here. He fits in. He looks comfortable, more comfortable even than he does at work.

He turns to look at me and takes a small step closer.

'I've been thinking about this,' he murmurs. He crosses

the room so that there is just a metre between us. Then, his voice barely above a whisper, 'About you.'

'I've thought about us too.'

I move towards him, now only a breath away from him. My hands are hesitant as I lay them on his chest. Time ticks by and we stay like that for a while, suspended in the moment. He breathes deeply, I feel him collect himself and gather his words.

'I-I'm sorry, Yara. To be honest I didn't know how to handle this feeling of… it's something I've never quite experienced before.' He places his hands atop mine, holding them still on his chest. 'And instead of dealing with it, I lashed out. Yes, when you thought the worst of me, it hurt. But if I'm being honest with myself, what have I ever done that would mean you could trust me? I know I can come across arrogant and competitive and ambitious – no wonder you could believe that I would steal your idea. And really, I… I was just using it as an excuse to push you away. But I…' He breathes in deeply. 'I don't want to keep pretending, Yara. I'm tired of pretending I don't have feelings for you.'

He's breathing heavily, as if the words cause him pain. Then, he sighs and smiles breathlessly, stands taller, relieved. He looks at me with eyes full of need.

'Xander, I feel the same way and I think that deep down I always have,' I say, my voice thick with emotion.

His face lights up and his face stretches into a broad, delighted smile. He puts his arms round my shoulders and pulls me into him. My face against his chest, I feel the warmth emanating from him. My heart swells so much that I can barely breathe with the pressure of it. In the last few weeks, I was so scared that this moment would never come. But now that it's here, I want to hold on to it tightly and never let it go.

Before I have a chance to say anything else Xander releases his hold on me slightly. He leans in and presses his lips gently on mine. Unlike the one in the storage cupboard, this kiss is soft at first, tentative, both of us exploring this new way of being together. Instead of urgent and desperate, this feels like we're establishing roots, laying the foundations for everything that's to come for us.

But then it's like a switch flips and the kiss becomes so much... more. I need it as much as I need my next breath. Our bodies fit together so perfectly, it's like we're born for one another. The kind of all-consuming, made-for-each-other romance that Xander said doesn't exist. But it must, because look at the two of us now.

We're both breathing heavily by the time we finally pull apart, but we don't let go of each other. Our foreheads touch, his hands cup my face, my hands are on his shoulders as we just drink each other in.

'You're incredible,' Xander rumbles. In the gruffness of his voice, his desire is evident. Which does something to me. But now is not the time... maybe once we get all the gooey emotional stuff out.

'I don't really know what to say. I'm just so, so happy.'

'You don't have to say anything,' Xander replies. My brain turns to mulch as his thumb gently caresses my cheek. 'I know exactly how you feel.'

As soon as the words fall out of his mouth, contentment settles over me and a smile tugs at my lips. In the end, everything we have been through, all the ups and downs, has been so worth it because they led us here.

'Not to jump straight back into *work stuff*,' I say and Xander grins down at me, 'but... seeing as you're here, maybe we should get the episode finished?'

'Together?' Xander asks.

'Always,' I reply. 'Because I love what you've done. But I do have notes.'

He chuckles. 'I wouldn't want it any other way.'

We work well into the night. We're on a roll, our ideas bouncing off each other so naturally. We improve and collaborate on the scenes we wrote separately. I suggest a line and Xander immediately finds the perfect retort. I work on the scene setting and the pacing, Xander questions whether a particular character would really do that. We knit the whole thing together, so it flows beautifully, one scene passing elegantly on to the next.

We do a final read-through to make sure it works. We perform the dialogue for one another – I laugh at Xander's terrible Irish accent and he's impressed by the gravitas I give Atticus. I don't even notice how late it has got by the time we're done. We sit back, exhausted. It must have been pure adrenaline that pushed us through the night. The episode is brilliant. It's everything I had hoped for and more. Everything that I—no, *we* had dreamed of. Yes, at the end of the day it's another episode of television. In our careers so far, we have contributed countless scenes and storylines to this show. But this episode is also a secret love letter to each other, and it will be signed with both our names.

We send the episode to Meagan and fall into bed. Our first night in this new stage of our relationship and we're too tired to do anything but sleep. But Xander holds me all through the night and, just before I drift off, I feel him place a gentle kiss on my forehead.

The next day Xander and I walk into the office hand in hand without a care in the world. As we progress through the corridors, we hear the whispered comments from our colleagues. Some are surprised… but most aren't.

We head straight to Meagan's office, and she looks up from her computer the minute we arrive. Her eyes zone in to our joined hands and a grin spreads across her face. 'If it isn't my two favourite writers. Oh, did I say that? Promise that you won't tell the others.' She quirks her head towards us and raises an eyebrow. 'Looks like you finally got your shit together… excuse my language.'

Xander and I look at each other.

'We did,' I say with confidence.

She stands from her desk. 'I knew I made the right choice pairing you two up.' She has printed the script and it sits pride of place in the middle of her desk. She glances down at it with a satisfied nod. She picks the papers up and brandishes them in her hand. 'This is an excellent piece of work. It's romantic and tragic and full of drama and pathos. It completes the characters' arcs while leaving us begging for another season. Genuinely, what a fantastic bit of writing, the fans and critics are going to devour it!'

She beams with pride. But then, she casts her eyes downward and her smile falters. 'I've been thinking about the question of lead credit... and whose name comes top.'

This is it. She's about to choose between me and Xander. Who did a better job. However, I realise that I honestly don't really care. Whatever she decides, we wrote something amazing and it'll open doors for us both, no matter whose name is on top. Xander squeezes my hand in reassurance and the gesture sends a zap of warmth into my heart. I know he feels exactly the same way.

'But reading this, I can't tell where one of your voices begins and the other ends – and so, I can't tell who did a better job. I confess, I only suggested it to try and get the best out of both of you. But if I'm very honest, it wasn't fair for me to put you both on this task and to make a judgement on who did more when you're both so incredibly talented. So, how about this...' She pauses. 'Instead of one of you getting top billing, how would you both feel if we just put it on one line? I know it's not our series style and the title designers will throw a fit about the deviation, but I think it's the fairest thing. If you'd be happy with that, of course!'

I can't contain my excitement. This is perfect. Yara Aslan and Xander Woods – our names will look so good next to each other, and hopefully will for years to come.

'We would absolutely love that.' Xander voices our shared agreement.

'Thought that might be the case.' Meagan claps her hands and ushers us out the door. 'Now get out of here, you two lovebirds!' she squeals with glee.

I give her a knowing look, thinking back to our conversation, and Meagan's grin grows wider.

As soon as we leave her office, swarms of our colleagues swamp us, eager to find out the outcome. *Did Meagan accept the episode? Who got top billing? Are you getting promoted? Or fired?* Xander and I just share a look and head back to our desks, ready for the next challenge.

Because in the end it doesn't really matter.

We have each other.

And that is enough.

Epilogue

Tonight is the night. The air is charged, carrying the hum of excitement that runs through the crowd. Leicester Square is abuzz with people, never a dull moment in the heart of London. They have really gone all out for the season finale watch party, decorating the Odeon with references to the show. I catch a glimpse of Layla's bejewelled tiara and the elaborate armour that Atticus wears. I see the lead actors ahead of me on the red carpet. Unlike the previous seasons, I've not arrived alone.

Xander and I walk down the carpet holding hands. It's been a year since we handed in our episode to Meagan. They filmed the show and we even got to go on set while our episode was in production. It was magical and grand, and it was incredible to see actors bring the words we wrote to life. The season so far has been greeted with critical acclaim and our viewership has grown even more. Everyone, like we predicted, is on tenterhooks to see how Layla and Atticus's arc will conclude in the final episode. And some of my favourite BookTokers are talking about the series! I've seen fan theories that one of them will die, that Layla is pregnant with her guardsman's baby, that Atticus will kill her. None of them have got it quite right.

But more importantly, this past year with Xander has been the happiest of my life. I didn't know if I'd be able to welcome someone into my heart again, but he's done it. We love to browse Lunar Books together after work – him with a black coffee and me with my chai. We spend our evenings reading, watching old movies and doing other, private stuff too... I sometimes can't believe we've finally got to this point of stillness after everything we have been through. It feels so right with him.

As we approach the mouth of the cinema and I think that soon everyone in there will be watching our episode, I feel the thrum of nerves simmering in my veins. I hope it goes down well. Tonight, we will finally get to see if all our hard work paid off.

Xander's arm is laced through mine and, with a slight nudge, he jolts me out of my anxious thoughts, 'You ready?' He peers down at me as if he knows exactly what I have been thinking. 'Everyone will love it.'

'I'm ready as I'll ever be.' I squeeze his hand to reassure him that I'm okay.

We head inside the cinema, where the seats are filled with an eager audience. I recognise critics from all the major publications and I pray that they'll enjoy it. There are also some devoted fans who are giddy with the excitement of being able to watch the series finale of their favourite show early, among the glitz and lights of the watch party.

At events like this, it's usually the cast, crew and some press ready to unleash their early reviews, but Meagan said we could invite our family and friends. I sit down next to Amira and wave at Andrew next to her – she finally dumped her loser boyfriend and he wasted no time asking her out. In fact, this is their first date – Andrew definitely knows how to impress a girl.

Maddie grabs my hand. 'Good luck! I'm so excited for you.' She pulls me into a deep hug and whispers in my ear, 'Do you think you can set me up with the hot actor y'all killed off in episode three?'

'I didn't kill him! It was the executive producers.' I laugh. 'But yes, I can try. He'll need someone to help him nurse his wounds.'

She squeals and squeezes me tight before running to take her seat again.

Xander holds my hand as the lights dim and the chatter falls to a hush as the long-awaited episode flickers to life.

Sometimes we get the chance to watch episodes early while they are in post-production, but Xander and I decided we would wait until this moment so that we could watch it for the first time on the big screen. Call us superstitious, but we thought it might be bad luck to see it any sooner.

Like a groom seeing a wedding dress before the big day.

We are seated with the rest of the script team and producers. As the iconic title sequence starts to play, I turn to look a few rows behind me and spot my parents and Elif sitting there, their faces unreadable in the dark room. I sent them the invite on a whim, not expecting their attendance, seeing as they have never come to any work-related event of mine before. I've spent years trying to explain to them how much this matters to me, but they've never understood it. But tonight, they have come, which means the world to me.

And suddenly, there:

Written by
Yara Aslan and Xander Woods

And clapping breaks out behind me. I turn again and see my parents and Elif cheering and gesturing wildly. Someone shushes them, but there's no stopping their smiles, which shine bright in the dark, illuminated by the screen. My dad waves wildly at me and Mum blows me a kiss. Elif puts a hand to her heart. She looks like she might be about to cry. I wave back at them, and turn round as the titles come to an end.

'My name's first, as it should be,' I whisper to Xander.

He throws his head back and has to stifle his exasperated laugh. 'It's alphabetical. And, *shh*, it's about to start.'

The entire room holds its breath in suspense as the finale

plays out on screen. Shocked gasps fill the room as Elaria is killed and the plot twist unfolds. Then, when Layla and Atticus finally kiss, the audience murmurs with delight. It's everything Xander and I hoped for and more.

Finally, when the screen fades to black, the room is silent for a few beats, which makes me slightly nervous. Xander's hand finds mine, offering me the comfort I need in this moment. *Oh God, they hate it after all.* I'm starting to panic when, all of a sudden, the sound of thunderous applause fills the cinema. I let out a breath of relief and look around with watery eyes.

Cheers and shouts of appreciation fill the space. Everyone who worked on the show, cast and crew alike, exchange emotional congratulations with each other. Awed, exhausted and grateful to have completed another successful season.

I stand up and start making my way to the exit, but then I feel a hand on my shoulder. My mum pulls me back and throws her arms round me. 'We're sorry, Yara, for ever doubting you... All of this' – she gestures with her hand – 'it's exactly what you're meant to be doing.'

'Told you so,' Elif says, nudging my mum.

'Elif was right,' Mum says. 'You were right, Yara.'

My dad nods in agreement, his usually stern face soft with understanding. 'We're really proud of you, Yazza Dazzler.' And there it is. The acceptance I've been craving for so long. It fills me with something golden and precious.

'Thank you,' I whisper. This time it's me who launches in for a hug.

I pull away and we chat for a while, all of them saying how much they enjoyed the episode, although my mum says it would be better without all the swearing. I'm filled with a feeling of belonging and contentedness, a sense that I'm exactly where I'm supposed to be with everyone I love most. Everyone except...

I take a look around the room until my gaze lands on Xander. I watch the exchange that he's having with Eloise, his sister. I let him have some time alone with her, as I know that's what he needs. He'd swallowed his pride and sent an invite to his parents, which I knew was difficult for him to do, giving them a last chance to have a relationship with him and take an interest in his life. But to no one's surprise, least of all Xander's, neither of them even bothered to respond. Eloise had come through for him, though, and that fills my heart with immense joy.

Xander's head peers over the crowd like a meerkat, his eyes searching and alert over the sea of heads. His brow starts to furrow until he spots me and his whole body loosens and his face breaks into a wide smile. He beckons me over towards him and Eloise. I wade through all the people, being stopped every few shuffles by an audience member who wants to wish me congratulations. When I get to them, Eloise is releasing Xander from a deep hug.

I'm close enough now that I hear the tail end of the

conversation. 'They don't deserve you anyway,' Eloise says. Her eyes are dewy with tears.

'It's okay. I've got everything I need right here,' Xander replies, as he places one arm round each of us.

We spend the night schmoozing. Other party-goers linger around us and we're constantly badgered by press asking about what the future may hold for us.

'Any exciting projects lined up, before the new season starts?' a journalist enquires, pen ready in hand, eager for some sort of exclusive. It doesn't escape me that some nearby conversations have quietened, keen to hear the answer. We look at each other. The glint of mischief that dances in Xander's eyes mirrors my own.

There is only one right answer. 'A rom-com,' we say simultaneously.

The crowd reacts instantly with burbles of excitement and intrigue. We had talked extensively about what we should do next, and we decided we really wanted to write something that would remind people of what it means to really *love* – the ups and downs of it all.

The night draws to a close and we slip away from the crowd, stepping outside to find a spot where it's just us.

I lean my head on Xander's shoulder, letting out a sigh. 'Can you believe we made it here... after everything?'

'Not to brag, but honestly? Hell yeah. We worked our arses off and it looks like it's finally paid off.' He lets out a deep chuckle.

'That it did,' I say, my chest puffing with pride.

He holds me close. We stand in the comfortable silence of two people who have no fear that one day the conversation will end. We'll always be able to pick up where we left off.

Then, Xander peels away from me slightly. 'Hey,' he says gently. 'I wondered if you had any idea for a title? For our rom-com?'

'Oh, I did actually. How do you feel about...' I pause for dramatic effect, '*The Ending is the Best Part*?'

Xander considers it for a moment. I watch nervously as he turns it over in his mind. He looks down at me and his eyes crinkle with happiness. 'I love it,' he says. 'I love you.'

'I love you too.'

It's quiet in Leicester Square now. Everyone from the watch party has gone on somewhere else. We'll join them soon. Xander grabs my hand and spins me once, twice under the glittering streetlights until we're both giggling. Then, he stops me and holds me by the waist. He looks down at me, his gaze full of that look of longing that I hope I never become used to. Xander presses his lips to mine and I return his kiss gratefully.

It's so perfect, you couldn't write it.

About This Book

The Ending is the Best Part was written by Lamia Zain as part of BookTok Made Me Write It. This project allowed TikTok users to vote on key aspects of the book, including plot points, character names and the cover. Thank you to everyone who participated in the votes – this book would not have been possible without you!

With generous thanks to all those who supported BookTok
Made Me Write It, including...

Isla J	Cat C
Toni M	Cassie B
Alyssa L	Hannah B
Andrea S	Rebecca B
Vibhuti P	Jamie-Lee W
Alexandra K	Izzy T
Sunbal M	Helen S
Laura S	Luutske P
River S-T	Danielle S
Amy R	Darcie T
Mollie S	Rachael B
Toluwani D	Michelle C
Kelly M	Rachel W
Pauline D S	Lorn F
Jo S	Halima B

Muskan G   Kirsti F

Gabby R   Yumna A

Mohsin H   Mary P

Becky P   Alice K

Rachel D   Zsanett S

Silvia L D   Nicole A

Katelyn B   Sarah B

Abdirahman M H   Elizabeth C

Daisy W   Evie M

Grace H   Freja M

Jessica G   Zeinab A

Melanie K   Davina T

Naomi S   Nicole C

Elizabeth C   Sarah B

Joanna O   Ally F

Jahaan K   ... and you!